# WHITE SHADOW

ROY JACOBSEN

# WHITE SHADOW

*Translated from the Norwegian by*
*Don Bartlett and Don Shaw*

BIBLIOASIS
WINDSOR, ONTARIO

First published in the Norwegian language as *Hvitt Hav*
by Cappelen Damm AS, Oslo, in 2015

First published in Great Britain in 2019
by MacLehose Press, London
an imprint of Quercus Editions Ltd
An Hachette UK Company

First published in North America in 2021
by Biblioasis, Windsor, Ontario

This translation has been published with the financial support of NORLA

Co-funded by the
Creative Europe Programme
of the European Union



FIRST EDITION
2 4 6 8 10 9 7 5 3 1

Library and Archives Canada Cataloguing in Publication

Title: White shadow / Roy Jacobsen ; translated from the Norwegian by Don Bartlett and Don Shaw.
Other titles: Hvitt hav. English
Names: Jacobsen, Roy, 1954- author. | Bartlett, Don, translator. | Shaw, Donald, translator.
Series: Biblioasis international translation series ; 35.
Description: Series statement: Biblioasis international translation series ; 35 | Translation of: Hvitt hav. | Sequel to: The unseen.
Identifiers: Canadiana (print) 20200406086 | Canadiana (ebook) 20200406124 | ISBN 9781771964036
(softcover) | ISBN 9781771964043 (ebook)
Classification: LCC PT8951.2.A3854 H8513 2021 | DDC 839.823/74—dc23

Readied for the press by Daniel Wells
Cover illustration by Joe McLaren
Designed and typeset by Libanus Press in Adobe Caslon

PRINTED AND BOUND IN CANADA

# WHITE SHADOW

# 1

The fish came first. Man is merely a persistent guest. The foreman came in and asked if any of the girls could split, there had been an unexpected influx of cod. Ingrid looked up from the barrel of herring and directed her gaze towards the quay, where dancing snowflakes melted into the black woodwork. She wiped her hands on her apron, followed him into the salting room and went over to the splitting bench and a tub of gutted fish. They looked at each other. He nodded at the knife lying there, it resembled a small axe.

She pulled a two-foot long cod from the rinsing tub and placed it on the bench, slit its throat, flipped up the gill cover and sliced through the ribs from the neck down to the belly and out to the tail, severed the backbone at the anus, cut through all the ribs on the right-hand side too, ripped out the spine as if she were undoing a rusty zip, and held it aloft in her left hand; the fish on the bloodstained bench looked like a white wing, waiting to be rinsed and stacked in layers, before being salted and turned and dried and washed and piled and sold, as the ivory-white gold that has sustained life on this scraggy coast for the eight hundred years that have passed since the place was first chronicled.

"Let's have a keek a' th' spine."

Ingrid switched it to her right hand to conceal the cut between her thumb and index finger. "Clien as a whistle."

He added that she could stay for as long as it took, you could never be sure in the autumn . . .

"But get s'm gloves on tha."

Ingrid looked down at her blood mingling with that of the fish and forming a drop that fell to the floor, as he turned his back and squelched over to the office on his rubber soles.

Ingrid longed to be gone, to be back on Barrøy, but no-one can be alone on an island and this autumn neither man nor beast was there, Barrøy lay deserted and abandoned, it hadn't even been visible since the end of October, but she couldn't be here on the main island either.

She split fish for ten hours a day, kept her distance from two salters and after a week couldn't sleep at night in the damp, chilly cooper's loft, where she lay with Nelly and two young girls from the mainland who were here because of the war. They pretended not to cry themselves to sleep, they gutted herring, boned them and salted them in barrels, added brine and drank ersatz coffee, salted and slept and washed themselves every other evening in cold water, their hair once a week, in cold water too, rust red beneath a starry firmament of glistening herring scales, and Ingrid split cod like a man.

In the middle of the second week one of the salters left and Nelly was sent to work with Ingrid. The following day was stormy and the fishing boats sought shelter in the islands. They didn't come in the next day either and when eventually they managed on the third morning to tack through the snow they didn't have a single fish in their holds.

But many people were waiting for them, a whole village was there to welcome men returning alive, once again. Then more bad weather, confined to harbour with idle fishing gear, catches that were of no value except perhaps for making guano, it depended on so much, especially the market prices in a different world from this; the sorted fish were tail-tied and hung, and the autumn's bizarre adventure was over.

Ingrid and Nelly turned over the salted fish, discarded the bad ones, ensuring that those at the bottom of the old pile were at the top of the new one. Now it was the end of the herring season, and the mainland girls were given notice, they received their meagre wages, picked the fish scales from each other's faces, washed each other's hair in cold water, dried and combed it, taking care to ensure their hairbands were straight before they left on the steamboat laughing and wearing clothes no-one had seen before.

With the same steamer came a letter – from Ingrid's aunt, Barbro, who was in hospital – set down on paper by a nurse whose handwriting was like a doctor's, a scrawl which Ingrid was able to read but did not understand. Her aunt wasn't coming up north because her upper femur was not knitting and because she couldn't get a lift . . . she would be back in good time for Christmas, she said twice, Barbro was fifty-nine and Ingrid thirty-five, that evening she soon fell asleep and had no dreams.

She also woke early and lay listening to the wind clawing at the slate roof and the sea gurgling and lashing between the posts beneath the quay and Nelly's breathing, Nelly's sleep was human, it was the only thing here that was as it should be, the sound of Nelly sleeping, night after night, now she couldn't stand it anymore.

Ingrid got up, washed in the galvanised bucket, packed her suitcase, didn't eat or make any coffee, carried her stinking work clothes down to the place behind the canning factory where the Germans burned rubbish, and tossed them into the oil drum, staring at the flames until people began to assemble on the quay, it was snowing lightly.

She went back and brewed some coffee of sorts, poured a cup and placed it on the chair by the bedhead next to Nelly, who still lay there looking like a serene corpse, waited for the reflection on the wall to tell her that the foreman had also arrived, that day was now dawning, though it was still dark, then got to her feet, went down to the office with her suitcase and said she wanted to settle up.

He placed his well-worn pencil on the desk, seemed

surprised, said she had caught him on the hop, he couldn't do without her, fish would be coming in that evening, he was sure of that, she was both necessary and surplus to requirements, the paymaster's usual convoluted trickery, but Ingrid was from an island, the sky was her roof and walls, so she repeated that she wanted her money *now*, and waited patiently for all the drawers to be opened and closed, all the papers to be shuffled, the ambivalent sighs over the time sheet and the equally laborious counting of the dog-eared banknotes, as though it were an insult to ask for your wages, as though on payday it were the master who was to be pitied, not the slave.

Ingrid walked up the icy road to the store and waited for Margot to open, selected the items she needed, including coffee and butter, paid with ration coupons and money, borrowed Margot's handcart, and wheeled her purchases down to the rowing boat, which had been moored beneath the quay all autumn.

She cleared the snow from the boat with a bailer, loaded her provisions and her suitcase, returned to the store with the cart and on her way back passed two German soldiers, who were sitting smoking on the sheltered side of the salthouse, they must have been there all the time, watching her.

She went down the steps, got into the boat, untied the mooring rope and sat at the oars. One of the soldiers came over to the quayside and shouted something to her, gesticulated, cigarette in hand, a red eye in the winter gloom. She rested on the oars and sent him a quizzical look. Again he shouted something she couldn't hear, the swirling snow thickened, the boat slipped away and the soldier vanished from view.

Ingrid rowed across to the elongated island of Gråholmen, following the sea-smoothed rocks at an oar's distance until they were gone, visibility was zero, the sea was heavy and calm.

From the marker on the last rock she steered a course, maintaining the angle between the boat's wake and the swell until she reached Oterholmen an hour or so later. The island was to port and it should have been to starboard. She adjusted her course, proceeded at a new angle between the swell and the twisting wake and reached Barrøy half an hour after she had lost sight of Oterholmen.

She unloaded her things, opened the boat-shed doors and hauled in the boat with the winch her father had installed when she was a child, straightened her back and looked around, the houses in the grey mass up on the island's humped ridge, visible at a distance of fifteen to twenty sea miles in clear weather, now just small, black boxes beneath a thin layer of milk, no light, no tracks in the snow.

She lifted the yoke onto her shoulders, hooked on her provisions and walked uphill. The boxes turned into houses and homes, surrounded by trees resembling charred fingers. She let herself in and went from room to room lighting the lamps, fired up the stoves in the kitchen and sitting room. She couldn't be here, either. She went back out, down to the boat shed, checked it was locked and moved the trestles to the leeward side, as though she hadn't done all this when she arrived. The bouldered harbour moles and the criss-crossed log skids in the green water, Oterholmen came into view and disappeared again. Not a boat to be seen. Not a bird. She turned and gazed at the houses, one with two yellow eyes, then she walked uphill for the second time, so now at any rate there were three sets of tracks in the snow.

# 2

The kitchen was warmer now. Ingrid took off her gloves and hat, ground some coffee and placed the pot on the stove, stocked the larder with her provisions, fetched more firewood and by now the coffee was ready. She took off her coat and drank the coffee, sitting in her own chair by the casement window, peering out at the shadows to the west, Moltholmen, Skogsholmen, Lundeskjærene and the sleepy shore, well into this day which would never come to anything. Still she did not eat. She looked around for a place to start, under the stove or the table, in the corner by the larder?

She got to her feet, pulled out the peat scuttle and began to tear the newspapers into strips, crumpled them into small balls and made a pile on the floor, like a snow lantern. It collapsed. She stacked them again, the newspaper was one she used to get in the days when Barrøy was a community, with people and animals and a lighthouse, with storms and doughtiness, with work, a summer and winter and prosperity, she laid some kindling and bits of peat around the balls of paper to make a fire, an idea no-one had had before, burning down a house on an island; there were some ruins on the eastern side of Barrøy, but no scorched ground, and suddenly there was no doubt anymore, those who had left Karvika had done so of their own free will, not because of any disaster, they had quite simply got sick of it, had looked at themselves in the mirror, packed their things and gone, it was an unbearable thought.

She grabbed a lamp and went up to the North Chamber, then into the South Chamber, poked her head into Barbro's room on the eastern side of the house, went into her own childhood room with a pull-out bed and a potty and a bedside table and faded school drawings, which she hadn't seen since she was here picking potatoes in September; the house had shrunk, the doors were lower, the windows narrower; the smell of its inhabitants had once stuck to these walls like paint, now all that was left was the odour of wet, heavy earth, she ran a fingertip through the beads of condensation and sat on her parents' bed where her mother had died.

"Let Lars take over Barrøy," was the last thing she had said. "And leave this place, you're young and bright, turn your back on the sea, heed my words . . ."

Ingrid said no.

"You're not strong enough."

"Yes, I am," Ingrid said to her dying mother.

The following spring Lars did not return from Lofoten, he had found love, he wrote, and stayed there with the boat and the crew and the tackle, year after year, even when war broke out.

And Ingrid and Barbro became lonelier and lonelier with every sun that rose and every storm that abated, with every animal they slaughtered and every sack of down they gathered and failed to sell, a young woman and a middle-aged woman on an island, waiting for letters from Lars, neat, regular ramblings, which one day were also furnished with some green scribbles, the signature of Lars' three-year-old son, Hans, the longest three years of Ingrid's life. Now the war had lasted for four, and Hans had a brother, Martin; with him came more scribbles, to an aunt and a grandmother who didn't write back because one of them was too proud and the other couldn't.

Ingrid went into the North Chamber and decided to sleep there, where a hatch in the floor led down to the kitchen, allowing the heat to rise. She shook and beat the eiderdowns, made the bed, went downstairs again and drank some lukewarm coffee as she re-read the letter from Barbro, whereupon she scrunched it up and placed it in the pile on the floor.

But she didn't set it alight.

She went into the sitting room to put some wood in the stove and noticed that her grandfather's bedroom door was ajar. She took hold of the handle, wanting to close the door, but she had done this a short time ago, she had shut the door and now it was open again, the house was silent, nothing stirred.

She heard a click, then distant, sustained thunder from the bowels of the earth, she backed into the kitchen and stood rooted to the spot, for much too long; then she returned and wrenched open the door and was angry with herself for not having done so in the first place, whoever it was could have got away.

But she could smell nothing, she heard no shuffling steps, mumbling voices or the sound of a cat, only the same faint hissing sound, inside and out. She unhooked the lamp from the sitting-room wall, went right inside her grandfather's room and established beyond all doubt that nobody was there, neither in the bed nor underneath it, neither in the corner cupboard nor in the chest, which she opened and closed, and sat on the lid with the persistent hiss of silence so loud in her ears that she had to scream.

Then the silence was total.

She put on her coat and went out into the falling snow, stopped and surveyed the buildings, the barn, then the quays and the boat shed by the sea, suddenly wonderstruck at all the things that had kept her on the island, which in truth were nothing at all. Soon the snow would turn to rain, the island would become as brown as scab and the sea grey, unless the wind changed.

Ingrid walked south through the gardens, avoided the gates and clambered over the stone walls as she did when a child. But she was a child no more. She continued to the southernmost point, where she stopped and stared at the ruins of the lighthouse, which she and Barbro had blown up with the last of her father's dynamite when war broke out, shattered glass in clear, garish colours, strands of seaweed and kelp wrapped like black hair around rusting, twisted iron girders, a paraffin drum resembling a scorched rose. She sat down on the tree trunk they had found drifting in the water and had secured with bolts and wires so that the sea wouldn't take it from them again, this colossal bone-white giant they thought one day would be worth something, maybe a fortune even, now it had served as a bench for three decades, for people who never sat down.

And Ingrid was no longer a child.

She waited until she began to feel the cold, walked north along the rocks to the west without seeing any footprints or hearing anything but the dismal wail of the sea, past the Hammer with the new quay and the three boat houses, that was at least one too many; she realised that if she had woken Nelly that morning, if she had allowed herself to hear her voice and see her smile, she would still have been at the trading post, tearing the backbones out of dead cod as her thoughts ebbed and flowed.

Standing in the new quay house, Ingrid bunched her wet hair and let it fall, repeated the action, wondering why she still wasn't hungry. She noticed a hole in the sleeve of her woollen jumper, was unable to remember how it got there. In a rectangular box on top of the workbench were some wooden floats arranged according to size. She took the largest and played with it, saw the teeth marks left by Lars, who chewed everything when he was a toddler. She still had dried fish blood under her nails. Her jumper had caught on a nail on the staircase as she went down with her suitcase that morning. On the shelf above the bench were spools of yarn of all dimensions, knives, whetstones, hooks, corks . . . and bodkins, Barbro's bodkins.

Ingrid pulled over the stool and sat by the iron hook beneath the window, threaded a bodkin and set to work on the gill nets. An hour later she had made three fathoms with a mesh size of fifteen. Her hands were soft and delicate in the cool air. She was ravenous, went out into the darkness of the night and back to the house, she had been wrong about the weather, the rain had turned to snow, as light and dry as soot, and she was no longer afraid.

# 3

Ingrid ate and slept and woke and was still not afraid. She took her time eating, dressed, went out into the fragile November light and pushed out the rowing boat. The wind had turned once again and had picked up, from the south-west. She rowed around the headland and into the metre-high waves, south through the sound to the anchor bolt which Lars had once hammered into a rock there, fastened a rope to the end without getting out of the boat – taking care not to let it dash against the rock – and rowed against the current across the sound to Moltholmen, where her cousin had also hammered in a peg, from which hung a pulley. She threaded the rope through the eye, again without getting out of the boat – taking care not to let it dash against the rock – and rowed back towards Barrøy, she had thought it would be eighty or ninety fathoms in length, but it was closer to a hundred and fifty, the line was too short.

She burst into tears, tied a float to one end and let it go, rowed north *with* the current to the new quay house to fetch more rope. The sea was rougher now. She fought her way out again and found the float, tied the ropes together and rowed back to the mooring on Barrøy with the end. She was soaked to the skin, sweating profusely, exhausted and furious, but now she had a line over the sound and could run a net, or two, fishing without recourse to a boat, in all kinds of weather, until the hardest frosts set in, perhaps even longer.

She let the boat drift north and put it away, noticed that the swell was falling and stopped short in surprise, she had expected it to rise, and still she wasn't afraid.

She went up to the house and slept on the bench next to the stove, not waking until it was evening. She felt cold and stiff, got up and put more wood on, cooked some food and wondered whether to set the nets in the darkness, dismissed the idea and opened one of the books she had, there was nothing in it.

She donned her waterproofs, walked to the new quay house and fetched two nets, walked south to the moorings by the sound and drew the first net, like a noiseless spider's web, into the black waves, fastened it to the eye of the second and kept pulling, two nets joined together, that wasn't much of a fleet, she pulled them fifteen fathoms further out, secured them and went home.

She slept naked in her parents' bed in the North Chamber, a long sleep, rose, another morning, pulled in the nets and had some fresh cod to cook, then went out and added another net to the fleet. Three. She could increase this to four or five. She had some dried fish left over from last winter, she had a cellar full of potatoes, there was some red saithe and half a barrel of herring. She had jam, flour, coffee, syrup, dried peas, butter from the store and sugar. Now she also had fresh fish. The pile of newspaper balls was no longer on the kitchen floor but in the wooden box beneath the stove, with the kindling. In a gap in the cloud cover two planes appeared, she heard gunfire directed at the Fort in the north of the main island, the gap closed again.

Next morning there were eight cod and one big saithe in the nets. She ate fresh fish again, and liver, and she salted the rest, sat in the warm kitchen looking around until something made her get to her feet and go to the hayloft above the cowshed, where the sacks of down were stored. From the first sack hung a label with Barrøy written on it. One kilo. 1939. She opened it and stuck her hand into a warm summer, then she closed it and undid the second sack. On this one the label said 1937. Another summer. She made up her mind to row to the main island and get a cat.

She went back to the house and put on the kettle, bathed and scrubbed her nails until the cuticles split, washed her hair, twisted it into knots before releasing it, felt the hot water running over her stomach and hips and thighs into the tub. She dried her body, dressed, then sat at the kitchen table and opened the same book. There was still nothing in it. But now she could sleep like Nelly.

She went to bed and thought about the cat. Soon Barbro would be here. The thought of Barbro. And Suzanne.

Suzanne had been like a daughter to Ingrid, but had left both her and Barrøy when no more than fourteen. She, too, had done so of her own free will.

Ingrid got up again and went down to the sitting room, where she took out the letters from the chest of drawers her father had once bought in a fit of madness, Suzanne's well-formed handwriting from the capital, where she had first served as a maid with a wealthy family, then worked as a telephone operator on a switchboard of considerable size and with an impressive name. Ingrid read slowly, swaying to the rhythm of the words, nodding, then she shook her head and put the letters down, visualising Suzanne the day she left the island in the finest clothes they had managed to muster, excited, joyous and as fragile as glass, she had not only taken her precious self but also all the island's savings, it had not been a pretty sight.

Ingrid blew out the lamp, went into the loft and slept like Nelly, after briefly turning her mind to Barbro again, and deciding that she would redeem the clock she had pawned at Margot's, the pendulum clock with roman numerals and ornamental hands, even an islander needs a silent dividing line between the two days that pass before a clock has to be wound up.

# 4

When Ingrid had been on Barrøy so long that even the thought of a clock had gone, a seal got entangled in the net furthest away.

She pulled the seal ashore and saw that it was dead. It was small, maybe a pup. She left it there for the eagles. But it had damaged large sections of the tackle, so she dragged the nets homewards to repair them, then she spotted another seal, which was lying in the snow, barely moving its flippers. She went closer. It looked at her through one black and one white eye. They'd had seals on the island before, but they were shy and took to the water when people approached. This one seemed limp and sickly and was no bigger than the dead seal.

Ingrid put down the nets, dug out a rock with her hands and killed it. Two eagles took off from Moltholmen and swooped down on her. She thrust an arm into the air, they recoiled, thrashing their massive wings, before landing back on the islet, where they sat cackling, eyeing her. One of them had an almost white head, the other was browner and slightly smaller.

Ingrid considered whether to skin the seal, but didn't know how to, and her father had said you had to be careful with seal meat, there might be trichina in it.

She was about to walk on, but as she lifted the nets she caught sight of some brown cloth beneath the snow, wadmal, it seemed. She pulled out a tattered shirt, and some wood shavings fell from it. Attached to the shirt with hemp twine was a pair of breeches, missing half a leg, and specked with more wood shavings. She had never seen clothes like these. She carried them to the fish-drying rack where she hung them up like ordinary washing, went to the quay house and stretched the nets between the pegs on the wall, picked out the seaweed and grass, and decided she had enough, so she could let them hang there and dry, then they were easier to repair.

She wondered whether to put out new nets, but decided she could eat salted fish for a few days yet, after which she made her way home in the lightly falling snow. A man was standing over by the rack looking at her, a man with one leg. Behind him the two eagles were tearing at one of the seals. The man seemed to be watching them too, it was difficult to see which way he was staring, this man with no head.

Ingrid went in, cooked some food and ate it, scrubbed the kitchen floor, the porch and the hallway, wiped down the stairs up to the loft, got out some wool and yarn, darned the hole in her jumper, realising that it hadn't been made by a nail at the trading post but by the splitting knife. In the morning she would do some baking, bread and *lefser* and potato *lefser*, a baking day, fill the house with the smells of a true home – and with bone-grindingly hard work.

She fetched a sack of wool from the barn and set about cleaning and carding it. She moved the spinning wheel into the kitchen and devoted the rest of the day to this. The rhythm. There was no longer any condensation on the inside walls. The smell of damp earth had gone. She had stopped lighting the fire in the sitting room. The calendar hanging from a nail in the larder, the cat she would soon be getting, the wall clock she no longer needed, the yarn running between her lanolin-softened fingers, and whenever she glanced through the window the stranger over by the drying rack was looking at her.

She wondered whether she should allow herself to get used to having him there, like a scarecrow, or else tear down the rags and throw them into the sea, bury them, burn them . . .

Before darkness fell she wrapped up, went out and felt them, they hung stiff in the frost, as if nailed there. Two dark patches in the snow, on the beach, where the seals had been. The eagles were nowhere to be seen. But she heard their cries, of other birds too, pulsating clouds of cosmic noise, which followed her into the quay house where she saw that the nets were dry and ready to repair. The cries of the birds followed her back home too, but now it was night and the man on the rack could no longer be seen.

# 5

To survive on an island you have to search. Ingrid had been searching since she was born, for berries, eggs, down, fish, shells, sinker stones, slate, sheep, flowers, boards, twigs . . . an islander's eyes are always searching, no matter what their heads or hands might be doing, restless glances across islands and the sea which fasten onto the slightest change, register the most insignificant signs, see spring before it arrives and snow before it daubs ditches and hollows with strokes of white, they see the signs before animals die and before children stumble and they spot the invisible fish in the sea beneath flocks of white wings, sight is the beating heart of the islander.

But when Ingrid went out this morning and saw from the weather that she wouldn't be rowing to the main island today either, she had a sense she was searching for something that couldn't be found, however hard, however intently she stared, it was like the feeling of making a mistake before you make it; and only the same jagged blankets of cloud gliding across the sky, releasing squalls of rain here and there over the restless sea, no life to be seen.

She walked south along the beaches in the east and found no seals and no clothes and was filled with a growing unease, which commanded her to talk aloud because sooner or later we need to hear a voice, even if it is only our own, every islander knows this, so she said out loud that she had to get this cat at all costs and started in surprise at the unfamiliar sound, repeated the words until they became ordinary and comforting, then she was stricken by further unease, the sense that she had lost her way on her own island, or that she was on a different island, or something even worse: the sense that she wasn't alone on this island of hers.

She had observed how quickly the eagles had torn the seals to shreds, she had seen the blood on the snow, which was covered by fresh snow, and resurfaced like a faint memory. She walked faster, trampled through a pile of seaweed and came across more clothes, rags, brown and wet, with clusters of wood shavings like the stuffing in a doll, though with differing stages of wear, as if they had belonged to different people, with different customs and lives. She spread the garments out on the snow, plus a cardigan and a jacket, and tried to match them as they must have belonged together, making *one* big person and two slightly smaller ones, and she had one item of clothing left over, half a person, and they were all men.

She stuffed the clothes into the string bag she always carried with her, intending to burn them at the northernmost tip of the island. But they were wet, and they couldn't be buried in the frozen ground either, so she hung them beside the man already on the rack and decided to walk all the way around the island again.

In the bay where she had found the first clothes, she spotted the eagles again, the white-headed giant and the smaller brown one, perched on a rock in the sea, beating their wings, pecking and clawing at each other as though fighting over prey.

But it was no rock, all around was open water, a hundred fathoms deep, and the rock was moving with the waves.

She ran out to the headland, was about to turn back to get the telescope, but slipped on a stone and caught sight of another rock where there shouldn't have been a rock either, and it too was moving, disappearing and reappearing like a driftwood log, a whale's back. And above them both hovered clouds of cackling, angry birds which converged and dispersed, dived and pecked and fought in a swirl of feathers and noise until every thing disappeared from view in a fierce snowstorm.

Ingrid covered her eyes with her hands and cried out. Nausea rose and her heart pounded, she had to get down on all fours, unable to breathe as she realised what she had seen.

She pressed wet snow to her face and ran home, passing yet more clothes, two whole outfits and a pair of breeches without a jacket, a torn grey cloak . . . swept them along with her as she ran through the gardens and hung them on the rack, made it to the house and lit all the lamps, also in the sitting room.

She stoked both wood stoves and stood in her dripping coat staring at a headless army on the rack, flapping in the soundless wind, one with one leg, one with one arm, a torso, two gaily fluttering cloaks, one without an arm . . . when it occurred to her that she had actually bothered with them because they were personal effects, no matter how torn and worthless they might be, and the wood shavings?

Ingrid went down into the Swedes' quay house and found the telescope, a heavy, extendable cylinder of something that resembled black moulded leather, with brass rings and two small focus wheels, she vaguely remembered that her father never used it because it distorted his vision, and now she decided she didn't need it anyway, she knew what she had seen.

She put down the telescope as if it were burning her fingers, fixed the two dry nets hanging on the pegs until her fingers were cold, then dragged them through the snow, tied the anchor rope to the eye of the first net and watched the cork floats bobble out into the waves, attached the smooth slate sinkers, careful not to crack them against the rocks, tied on the next net and pulled, two nets, the usual fifteen fathoms from land, then her eyes rose from the line and the sea to Moltholmen and she saw the first body.

The line slipped from her hands, she plunged into the sea and grabbed hold of it, waded ashore and fastened it, placed the palms of her hands on her knees and straightened her back, stared across the sound and still saw what she saw, what she had seen the previous day, yet she had slept like Nelly nonetheless.

She smacked her mittens together and saw the man lying half way up on the rock with his legs dangling in the sea as though someone had moored him to the anchor peg.

But the sea was falling and he would soon be on dry land, until the next high tide lifted him loose again and carried him away, and flocks of screaming harpies would dive down and tear at this brown figure.

Ingrid walked north to the boat shed and reflected that she had been to the barn loft twice, once to check the sacks of down and once to fetch some wool; there, too, she had seen something without understanding what it was, and she had left the house countless times, but had not been round at the back where the fruit bushes were, they never went there in the winter, who would ever think of walking around their own house . . . ?

She ran past the fish rack and over the marsh, hesitated before opening the porch door, went in and stood stock still in her own home, then ran with the blood pounding in her ears from one room to the next and paused and ran out again, around the house, and saw the tracks just visible beneath the new snow, as though someone had dragged a sack through the garden and up the barn bridge.

She walked up and confirmed the doors were locked with the bolt drawn on the inside, she ran around the building and into the cowshed and remembered she had seen drops of water on the steps, thinking they had come from a leak in the roof, climbed up into the hayloft and in the dim light she saw two legs sticking out from under some old sheepskins. She pulled the skins aside and saw a middle-aged man, bald, with bluish-black bristles in a wasted, chalk-white face, a dead man. But someone had closed his eyes and arranged his hands on his chest, as though praying.

She went further in and caught sight of another man, under two sacks of down and an old horse cloth. She pulled it off him and saw he was wearing the same brown rags, padded with the same wood shavings that spilled out of the sleeves and holes, and above all this a uniform with badges and stripes, a German uniform; he, too, was hollow-cheeked, bald and lean, but he had no bristles, he was too young, and he was alive.

# 6

Ingrid knelt down and tugged at him. He didn't react. Through a rip in his trouser leg, at the top of his right thigh, she saw a deep wound with edges that had swollen to form thick, blue lips. She pressed her fingers against them, saw living blood and heard a distant groan. One of his hands looked as if it had been burned in a fire, but most of the fingers were intact, the nails on the other hand were missing, it too was black.

Ingrid wrung a few drops out of the uniform and tasted them, it wasn't salt water, so there had to be a boat somewhere around the island, moored presumably in the only place she hadn't looked, near the ruins at Karvika, she was afraid of the ruins at Karvika, she always had been.

She managed to raise him into a sitting position, went down on her haunches and locked her hands around his chest, discovered how surprisingly light he was and dragged him over to the barn door, unbolted it and lugged him through the garden and into the kitchen, manoeuvred him up onto the bench, and covered him with blankets.

She grabbed the ladle in the bucket, propped him up and moistened his cracked lips. He writhed and groaned. She shoved a cushion under his head and fetched a funnel, stuck it down his throat until he retched and forced open his singed eyelids and tried to resist with his hands.

She held the ladle in front of his wild eyes.

He nodded, drank a few drops, coughed and raised his mangled hands as if to study them, and display them to her, or to God, as soot-blackened tears streamed from his scorched eye-sockets down his skeletal face, finding nowhere in his smooth, young features to stop them, making him look as if he had never been human, nor ever would be.

She grasped the hand missing only fingernails, sat holding it, staring into space, when she suddenly felt an imploring tremor, as if he were preparing to die. She began to shake the limp body, shouted no, no, grabbed the ladle and forced more water down him, causing more fits of retching, which eventually abated, reducing him to a whimpering infant, and the stench that permeated the warm kitchen was unbearable.

She got to her feet, went into the larder and stopped in front of the rows of shelves stacked with preserves and canned food. She grabbed a jar of redcurrant jelly and spooned the contents into a cup, mixed it with warm water, breathing through her mouth, and began to force a thin, red liquid down him. He coughed and spat and had to gulp to avoid choking, managed a few greedy gulps, brought them up again, swallowed a few small spoonfuls, she counted them, and he kept them down, until he passed out.

Ingrid placed the cup on the table, wiped her face on her jumper, heard two sobs, which were her own, and declared in a loud voice to the walls that this could not be true, before once again making sure that he was breathing, whereafter she went out into the driving snow and stared up into the darkness.

Only to realise that there was no way out of this.

She walked down to the landing stage and put out the boat, rowed around the northern promontory, where she had the wind in her face and kept beneath the jutting rock face, headed south through the foaming breakers to the fleet of nets, where the cries of the birds above Moltholmen were carried to her on the wind.

Using the last reserves of her strength she crossed the sound and jumped ashore, the boat left pitching against the rocks. She bound the mooring rope around her wrist, grabbed an oar and thrashed out at the swarm of screeching birds. The dead man came into view with a bluish-black hole for a face and his belly agape like a gutted cod through to the spine, his hands gnawed-off stumps of bone and his feet resembling charred wood. She slung the oar back into the boat, managed to lift him clear of the anchor peg and down into the seaweed, but not onto the boat. She wrapped the mooring rope around his thigh, leaped aboard and towed him along beneath clouds of birds making wilder and wilder dives into the wake. But now she had the wind at her back and sped along until, sheltered by the quay house, she was able to untie the mooring rope at the bow, step onto the quay and attach it to the hook on the windlass and hoist the man free of the water; he hung upside down like a man on the gallows.

The white-headed eagle stood on the quay beside her like a tame animal, she kicked out, it waddled away, she kicked again, screamed and lost her grip of the winch, caught it again and locked it into position, grabbed a wooden pole and lashed out wildly at the enormous bird, which lazily waddled to one side. She ran back to the windlass and lifted the man the last few metres up onto the stone quay, opened the doors of the quay house and dragged him inside, whereupon she discovered that one of his trouser legs was empty.

She closed the doors, shrieked at the swarm of cackling birds that had settled on the quay and the windlass and the roof, walked down to the boat and rowed back to the shed. She found herself crying and realised she had been doing so ever since she left the house.

She wiped her face on her drenched jumper, walked up the hill and again into the stench that filled her kitchen like intense cooking fumes and saw that the cup of redcurrant jelly was empty.

She tore off her jumper, tied a headscarf around her mouth, removed the blankets and began to undress him.

Beneath the uniform were the same brown rags, wood-shavings and an indefinable grey mass resembling sodden paper. She picked it all off him like dead skin from a sunburnt back, cloth, skin, soot, mould, and stuffed it into the stove, almost smothering the flames. She put in more wood and the temperature rose as he screamed in a voice that was not human.

Then she had to throw up before she could continue.

When he lay naked before her, black, pink, yellow and bluish-green, like a charred map of the world, she poured lukewarm water into a bowl and set about washing those parts of him that were unscathed; he moaned and struck out at her. She had to sit on him, and also removed something from him she could not identify, was it underwear or burned skin? He passed out again and lay motionless like a corpse, but still breathing.

She carried on until she was finished, filled the stove with the rest of the rags, went upstairs to the South Chamber and came back with an eiderdown and a new rug, slipped the rug under him and laid the eiderdown over him, opened all the windows and doors, filled all the saucepans she had with water and put them on to boil. She fired up the stove, hotter than on any baking day, while reassuring herself time and again that his slumber was not the sleep of death.

In a frenzy she tore off her own clothing, and burned that too, washed her body, put on some dry clothes, and the stench was no less abominable.

She pulled the eiderdown off him and began to wash him again, rubbed the thin skin, which in places was as smooth and white as a cod's belly, fetched some talcum powder and burn ointment, and a needle and thread, heated the needle over a candle and began to sew the gash in his thigh. Tremors spread through his frail body, but he still had a pulse, regular, and kept groaning until she put down the needle and bandaged the wound.

She shut the windows, went into the sitting room and looked at herself in the mirror above the chest of drawers, smacked her stiff, unrecognisable lips, then went back and sat down, alternately looking at him and down at her own hands, they were swollen and puffy due to the water and frost, but they were not shaking, and when she opened her eyes again she was lying curled up on the floor next to a stove that had gone cold in a kitchen without light, and outside there was silence.

She rolled over onto her back and lay listening to the calm, regular breathing on the bench, the night beyond the window panes was black.

She got to her feet like a stranger to herself, pulled off the eiderdown and stood gazing at him, covered him again, lit the stove and dressed to go out and look for the boat they must have arrived in and found it where she knew it would be, on a low-lying spit of land at Karvika, an oval, dirty white craft made of planks and metal cylinders, more a raft than a boat, probably visible through binoculars from the main island, in daylight and clear weather at any rate. Now it was dark, but the stars were out, so she couldn't burn it, nor would she be able to drag it over the crag and out of sight either.

She sat down.

It was quiet. No birds. She got up and spotted some drain plugs in the tanks, managed to loosen them and push the boat back into the sea and loaded it with rocks, launched it with her feet and watched it fill with water and sink like a white shadow.

Now only the lustreless stars were reflected on the surface, she had forgotten her mittens and couldn't move her fingers.

Back at the house she took off all her clothes again and inspected every inch of her body, as if looking for lice, then scrubbed herself until her skin was red and sore, until she was both hot and cold; she went into the sitting room and stared in the mirror, her face was dry and her body wet.

She dried her body and put on some potatoes and fish, overcooked them and mashed everything together, mixed in some liver and began to feed him.

He fell asleep.

She laid a hand on his wound.

He opened his skinless eyelids and peered at her with pupils like jellyfish in a black sea. She showed him the spoon, he nodded and opened his mouth, she fed him and he sucked and managed to swallow. She gave him another spoonful, and another, and warm redcurrant jelly, he coughed and drank, was given more and passed out in mid-mouthful. She wiped his chin, put a hand first on his forehead, then on his neck, to feel for a temperature and a pulse, and kept it there for so long that it seemed like a caress, then withdrew it and stared at it and stroked his chin twice more because it was impossible not to. Then she ate the rest of the food and went upstairs and fell asleep, fully dressed.

# 7

Ingrid had a feeling of water. It ran into her ears and filled her thoughts – with words. She felt the weight of eider down and her own body heat; her hands no longer ached, they weren't even red, her throat was dry, she said nothing and the foreign words continued to stream upwards from down below through the hatch in the floor.

She sat up, thrust her feet into the woollen lugg boots and went downstairs, but not into the kitchen, instead she put on a jumper and went out to fetch wood. The sky was grey, the light snow was falling gently, not a boat to be seen on the sea, but still the sound of birds, and again the screams, they came from within.

She went into the kitchen and the smell told her she would have to wash him once more, she took her time lighting the stove while he watched through a veil of fever and kept repeating the foreign word in a voice that was strangely deep for such a young man, now at least they were human sounds.

When at last she dared to look straight at him he stretched

out the hand lacking only nails, and hid the other. She sat holding it until his eyelids drooped again. Then she washed him the way a human should be washed, it took time, she cried, ate, waited, the silence outside, the snow was becoming thicker and thicker, and he slept peacefully.

When it could be deferred no longer, she wound three scarves around her face and went to the south of the island with a sheath knife and one of her father's old spritsails, followed the sounds and found the first one by the Russian tree trunk, he looked no more human than the body she had found on Moltholmen. She chased the birds away, cut a chunk off the sail and covered him, placed rocks on the corners and wondered what she would do if she found a woman.

The next was on the headland where she had stood watching the moving rocks. She covered him with sailcloth as well. The third lay directly south of the mooring line she used for the nets. She covered him with sailcloth and rocks and walked past the fleet of nets without looking down into the sea and found the fourth outside the Swedes' quay house. In her schooldays Ingrid had read about mission fields and dreamed of saving the living, now she was saving the dead, husks emptied of their contents by maggots and birds. She wondered what made them float, supposed there must have been a shipwreck, some disaster, that day she was in her grandfather's room, her ears filled with a sound she had never heard before, which stirred a strange fear in her because she nevertheless knew what it signified.

*

She went to the boat shed and pushed out the rowing boat, gathered the earthly remains in a netting bag and towed them to the quay, winched them up amidst a tornado of birds, then dragged them into the new quay house, where she covered them with old hemp sacking, wondering what would happen if there were prolonged mild weather and what she would do if she found a woman.

She went up to the house, again avoiding the kitchen, found her father's old Krag rifle, took one of the rugs from her grandfather's bed and settled into a prostrate position on the ground outside and aimed at the slate boat-house roof, which was black with birds, fired one shot after the other, reloaded and pointed the barrel at the white-headed giant sitting on one of the ridges. A black wing spun into the air and disappeared, a flock of seagulls and ravens and crows swirled into the grey sky, wheeled and dived back down. Ingrid reloaded and fired. Another wing spun into the air, one of a small eagle, two ravens, one black-backed gull; she realised the wind was a westerly, so the reports would be audible on the main island, now she had also shot to pieces the precious slate roof, she continued until she had run out of ammunition, got up and shook the snow off the rug.

When she went into the kitchen he was standing naked on thin, rickety legs, holding the edge of the table with the nail-less hand, and again he hid the other behind his back like a badge of shame – and stared at her in terror.

She showed him the gun, put it in the corner, and realised that she still had the scarves wrapped around her face, she peeled them off and told him to sit down and show her his burned hand.

He seemed not to understand.

She shoved him onto the bench and grabbed his hand, which wasn't a hand but a black foot with five toes and no nails. She removed the charred fragments from the rug with a cloth and threw it in the stove, fetched some gauze bandaging and ointment, which she applied to his hand, then bound it as he wept soundlessly and stared at the window.

She told him that unless she was much mistaken, an easterly was on the way, so she could row over to the main island to see what had happened, fetch help . . . He repeated the foreign word, like an echo from the morning, and now she thought it sounded like *mama*.

She caught his eye, pointed to herself and said Ingrid. He nodded and looked down at his bandaged hand. She waited for him to look up, then pointed at him and asked him what his name was. He placed the white bundle against his chest and said Alexander. Ingrid nodded, said Alexander and smiled and repeated Ingrid, Ingrid and Alexander, as if to establish an incontrovertible fact, got up and mixed some redcurrant jelly and hot water and placed the cup in front of him and watched as he balanced the cup between the heels of his two hands and drank and wiped his mouth with the bandage and repeated "Ingrid" with great solemnity, as well as the word she thought must mean *mother*.

Alexander, Ingrid said.

She said that both his hands would get better, at any rate, he would be able to use them, for something.

He gazed into space, unable to understand.

She repeated what she had said. He nodded and stared at the window pane, which resembled a thin layer of ice. She boiled some more fish and potatoes and fed him when he indicated he couldn't hold the spoon. She had something to eat herself, and took out the coffee mill, placed it between her knees and for the first time perceived a slight smile on his handsome face, the aroma of precious coffee in a kitchen and the sound of beans being ground. Ingrid had never seen whiter teeth and reflected on the uniform he had been wearing over the rags. She started asking him questions, which he didn't understand.

She pressed him, he mumbled a few words, and they didn't sound German. She asked him where he came from and how old he was and heard other words by way of an answer, they too were repeated, so she decided they must mean: I don't understand.

There could be many reasons for him to be wearing a German uniform. Such as?

Ingrid got up, put the coffee into the kettle and waited until the grounds rose like a gas bubble in black mire and burst, then she lifted the kettle and banged it hard, twice, on the stove rings and poured out two cups, but didn't place one in front of him. She put her own to her lips and drank, keeping her eyes on him as she asked if he wanted some coffee and heard him answer:

"*Da, spasiba.*"

She gripped the cup and asked him again if he wanted some coffee, he looked right and left, irritated and exhausted, as he repeated the two words and said something else, which didn't sound German, either.

She gave him the cup.

He placed his white bundle on the table and knocked the cup over. She apologised, wiped the table and re-filled his cup, squeezed onto the bench, behind him, so that he had to lean back against her and she put the cup to his lips. He twisted his head, glanced up at her in surprise and slurped down some coffee while she became aware of the presence of a man in the house, and that there was no longer the slightest trace of that terrible stench. They sat like this to the sound of staccato breathing, as though she had never been a woman before, and could now allow herself for the first time to be filled with the overwhelming certainty that a different island did exist.

# 8

The wind had shifted to the east, and the weather had cleared. But Ingrid didn't row to the village. She walked around the island with the sheath knife and her father's old spritsail, following the flocks of birds and finding several nameless bundles, slimy, mutilated masses, which once had been joy and sorrow, with cobalt-blue sludge in gaping eye-sockets the size of fists, spongy, yeast-coloured dough, and bones that were green from the sea and salt, rotten flesh, algae and hagfish.

She covered them and laid rocks on the sail corners, walked the long way north, fetched the rowing boat and towed the bodies to the quay and hoisted them up, oblivious to whether she was freeing the island of the monster of the deep or because all death makes demands that have to be obeyed.

She had the shotgun with her, rested the oars at regular intervals and fired a flurry of shots, causing the flock to explode and rise like a mushroom to the sky before falling again and enveloping both her and the boat and what she was towing in an impenetrable frenzy of noise and wings – now the wind would definitely carry the shots seawards.

She went home, undressed, burned her clothes and washed without shame in front of his coal-black eyes, which yesterday, or was it the day before, she had felt drawn to like no others, and of which she now knew she would never get enough, that was what gave her strength, she had never been stronger.

She cooked some food and they ate, she sitting on a chair, longing to go back to the bench and his body. She made some coffee, and each of them drank in silence, until she had to get up and go to the loft to find something for him to wear, her father's old clothes, which she began to try on him, her fingers against his body, he looked like a young boy on his first fishing trip, a fisherman, a skipper, a farmer and a pioneer.

They chuckled, he pointed at himself and said Alexander and at her and said Ingrid, he never tired of these words, and nor did she. Then she undressed him again and clipped his toenails, held his unscathed marble white feet and slowly washed him as they each spoke their own language and understood every word.

Before night fell, she went around the island again with the gun and pieces of sail and found what she found, went home, undressed and burned another set of clothes and stood naked in front of him and scrubbed every inch of her body. She washed her hair, and her body again with several changes of water, and combed and plaited her hair, and he didn't say a word and didn't take his eyes off her; after they had eaten, she said he should get up and walk, could he walk a few steps?

He struggled to his feet and shuffled towards the window, then to the larder, turned and grimaced, not without some silent laughter, and looked down at his bare feet. He walked to the hallway door and back to the window, stared at his own reflection, stepped back, turned and looked at her in despair, until she got up, took him by his bandaged hand, led him into the hallway and up the stairs into the North Chamber and lay with him for the rest of her life.

# 9

Ingrid made a hideaway out of the closet behind the door. It was flush with and indistinguishable from the wood panelling in the South Chamber and resembled a downy nest. And as he could walk without difficulty now, she led him out into the darkness, waited while he sat on the lavatory and heard him talking through the open door. They walked south through the gardens without a word, but she could hear him weeping. She pointed to the sky and the northern lights, unwonted cascades of rainbows at the wrong time of year, recited the names of pitch-black mainland mountains, taught him the words water, wind, snow, grass, of which there was none, seaweed, boat, fish, cat . . .

One evening she took him to the barn loft and pulled the horse cloth off the dead man and asked who he was, she had laid the uniform over him.

He didn't look at the huddled-up mummy, but muttered Alexander twice. She looked at him in surprise.

He said Sasha.

She held up the uniform and asked if they were friends and

had the same name. He nodded vigorously and shook as if indicating the cold, and she thought he must have stolen the uniform to keep warm, realising at once that also the wood shavings meant warmth and that they, too, suggested he was a Slav. She asked whether he was Russian and he said *Da*, but only after she had repeated the question three times. She asked if he was a soldier and he answered yes and no, she had never felt more attractive, and she stopped asking questions.

She got him onto the stern thwart in the boat, where he sat like a terrified landlubber while she rowed through the sound between the island and Moltholmen and loosened the anchor lines on both sides of the sound. They towed the nets after them in the silvery wake, lifted them and dragged them onto the quay without seeing what they were doing. But there were no birds now. And she tried to console him.

They walked home, undressed each other, washed each other and lay in the North Chamber like husband and wife. Ingrid didn't give a thought to her childhood, her parents, Barbro, Suzanne, Lars, everything she had missed, all the things she herself had messed up and destroyed, it felt as if she lacked for nothing.

She mumbled to the roof beams that tomorrow she would row to the main island, buy some food, get a cat and find out what had happened.

She could feel from his arm that he was nodding.

She asked if he understood and decided he did.

She said cat and meowed. He said Koshka and she could feel his smile against her fingertips. She ordered him to stay in the hideaway she had made and not to leave whatever he heard, shots or screams, he was to lie low from the moment she closed the door to the moment she opened it again, it might be a few hours, half a day at most. He said *spasiba* and cat and hideaway.

Ingrid thought she had everything under control when she hoisted the sail and glided over to the main island in the thick drifting snow, filled with hope that she could rid Barrøy of mortal remains and suspicion, a hope only the occupying forces could realise, if she played her cards right.

She moored as usual below the trading post, ran up to the village noticing not only an unaccustomed stillness, but that some of its fundamental essence had been ripped away by force, guards, vehicles, horses, an emptiness caused by something she was unable to put her finger on.

In the store she heard from Margot that British planes had sunk a German troop carrier a few miles further south. Hundreds had been killed, maybe thousands.

Ingrid said:

"Hva?"

Yes, Margot had heard about it from her son, who delivered goods to the Fort at the north of the island.

"War thar soldiers aboard?" Ingrid said.

"That's hva they seid."

"German?"

Margot said yes, and her expression changed, she scrutinised Ingrid's face, and Ingrid was no longer in control of matters; she asked if the camp behind the school had been abandoned. Margot said most of them had moved to the Fort, where the radio, the P.O.W. camps and the artillery positions were, but the Kommandant is here today.

Ingrid blinked and looked around. She asked if Jenny and Hanna still had any cats.

Margot said that was probably all they had, this mother and daughter, with whom Ingrid had salted herring since she was a young girl and who lived in a grey cottage north of the canning factory.

But when she left the store, her unclear mission faltered again, then she strode up to the camp behind the school, where she was stopped by a uniformed guard. She said she had to speak to the duty officer. He squirmed and said in broken Norwegian that this was not possible.

Ingrid said *Tote Tote* and flashed the fingers of both hands twice.

He lit a cigarette and stepped up close to her, made a few menacing gestures and fired off a tirade of searching questions, of which she understood not one word.

She repeated *Tote Tote* and held up her fingers again.

He huffed and glowered in the direction of some barracks at the other end of some open land, said "Follow me", and took her to an office that was so hot it almost took her breath away. A bald, middle-aged officer was entrenched behind an imposing desk, a man with a blond moustache, a pink scar across his face and large, artless eyes, a man who was about to poke a spoon that was far too big into a boiled egg, while talking excitedly into a telephone receiver.

He looked up at her and nodded angrily at a chair.

Ingrid sat down and stared with fascination at the spoon in the hairy fist, it resembled a buoy, while the officer continued to talk on the phone as if she weren't there and the soldier saw his chance to escape.

Eventually the officer rang off and shifted the spoon into his other hand. Ingrid repeated *Tote Tote*, again using her fingers, told him where she lived and said she needed help. He appeared to understand what she was talking about, shook his head as if to rid himself of some discomfort and said, "*Jawohl*, they had been struck by a disaster, *eine riesige Katastrofe. Die Leichen sind überall auf den Inseln.*" There were bodies everywhere.

Again Ingrid had the feeling she was searching for something that didn't exist, a chill ran through her and she asked for permission to go. He blinked:

"*Selbstverständlich. Ich hab' Sie nicht eingeladen.*"

Of course. I didn't invite you here.

She staggered out into the cold and walked down to her boat, but by the canning factory she made a sharp turn north and entered Hanna and Jenny's hot, ashen-grey kitchen, greeted them and said she had heard they had some kittens.

Hanna said yes, they did, and told her to sit down, to take it easy, Ingrid didn't look well.

With a brief laugh Ingrid asked what she looked like then, realising she couldn't say anything about the bodies here either, as though she couldn't trust them, these people she had known all her life, as if they were from a different island. Hanna looked down at her knitting and asked if it wasn't lonely out there now, on Barrøy.

Ingrid said yes, it was, that was why she wanted a cat.

Wouldn't she rather stay with them for a while until Barbro returned?

And now Hanna looked straight at her again.

Ingrid said it wasn't certain Barbro would be coming back.

Hanna looked dubious, but shouted into the adjacent room.

They heard Jenny's voice and the clatter of doors. It was a clean, freshly scrubbed home, the chimney didn't draw properly, there was a hiss under the washing boiler. Hanna said they had kept this kitten because of the checked pattern on its back, was Ingrid hungry?

Ingrid said she didn't want to eat others out of house and home.

Jenny came with the kitten in a basket, over which she had placed a piece of herring netting so that it could stick a paw through the mesh. Ingrid held it in her fingers and asked what its name was.

"Hva tha likes," Jenny said, before she too started studying her face, wouldn't Ingrid like to stay there for a few days?

Ingrid smiled, said no, thank you, and left, hurried back to the store, as if there was hope yet, someone she could tell, in any event she needed to buy some items, and that was as far as she got, then she remembered she also wanted to redeem the clock, would Margot take ration coupons instead of money, for the time being?

Margot asked what in heaven's name she should do with ration coupons.

"But just teik it. It's not worken'."

She went into the storeroom and fetched the pendulum clock, wrapped it in sacking and rolled the weights in a towel, put everything in the box of provisions and Ingrid walked out with a double-edged relief – it was like nausea – and down the road and clambered aboard the færing; she placed the basket with the cat inside on the stern thwart, as on a throne, between two net sinkers so that she could keep an eye on it during the journey.

The wind was still coming from the south-west, she had to row, initially at an angle to the waves, then head-on, the swell had never been greater and the day never shorter. She rowed too fast, became agitated and sweaty, rowed even faster and the sea splashed into the boat. In the lee of Oterholmen she had to bale water and drifted north. She rowed too fast again – the cat yowled beneath the spray from the sea – and rammed the landing stage on Barrøy only after navigating through waves that became smaller and smaller the closer she came to the island, and by then it was dark.

She ran up with the basket and lit the lamps in the kitchen and sitting room, lit the stove, then went upstairs, took a deep breath and opened the closet door, holding the cat in front of her like a shield.

He slumped like a sack in the sudden light. Ingrid stood there without speaking. He reached out for the kitten, said Koshka and smiled, and rubbed his nose against the kitten's.

Ingrid asked if he was German, *Deutsch* . . . ?

He didn't understand.

Distraught, she told him that a German troop carrier had been bombed and noticed he had removed the bandage on one hand, he must have used his teeth, his skin was healing, his fingernails looked like tiny pink shells.

She called out something she didn't understand herself, went down and out again and put the boat away, carried the box of provisions back up and in the kitchen frenetically began to make a length of netting, which she suspended from the edge of the vent in the ceiling. The kitten climbed up a few feet and hung by one claw, let itself down again and sat meowing and striking out with both paws while Alexander smiled quizzically, at her – was his name Alexander?

She went upstairs and lowered the yarn netting, the cat sank its claws in it, she lifted it all the way up, it looked around the North Chamber, she carried it down into the kitchen again, went back up, repeated the process and Alexander clapped in silent acknowledgement as the cat at last realised it had been given a ladder.

Ingrid said she was going to call it "Koshka".

He corrected her, pronounced the word twice and said *ja, ja*, when she got it right.

But she didn't smile.

She asked him whether he was German or Russian.

He wrapped his arms around her, again she saw the far too small egg and the large spoon and began to scream and pummel him with her fists. He managed to push her down onto the bench and sat on her, speaking a language that still didn't sound like German. Then he began to sing, a children's song, which didn't sound German either, lay down beside her and breathed in her ear until their breathing harmonised and neither of them spoke.

Ingrid buried her fingers into his short, black hair, sniffed and smelled only soap, kissed him and said he had to fetch some wood, she didn't have the energy, she was dead, did he understand what that meant – dead?

He smiled and pulled on a jumper, went out and came in with wood and peat as if he lived there and stoked the fire as if he lived there, whoever he was, and he stood looking at her, he was such a shiningly beautiful monument of a young man that she had to look away.

Then he said something she interpreted as a question, and she nodded.

He began to cook some food, humming the same children's song while mixing dough and rolling it into plate-sized round shapes and adding bits of cold, boiled fish and butter, folded them over like fat pancakes on a tray and put them in the oven.

He lay down beside her and let her do what she wanted with him as an unfamiliar smell spread through the room. They ate in silence, went to the loft and lay there together until the first storm hit the southern wall.

Ingrid said through her tears that now they didn't need to get up. No-one would be coming to the island.

They fell asleep and lay at each other's side the whole of the next day, and the night thereafter, listening to the weather and getting up to eat and play with the cat; the storm forced them to shout, even those things which should only have been whispered.

After the storm abated she asked if he could repair a clock.

He said yes and asked if she had any tools.

She said she had already shown them to him, didn't he remember?

He looked at her questioningly.

She repeated "tools" and explained where they were. He nodded energetically and laughed, wrapped the eiderdown around him, went down and didn't reappear.

So Ingrid also got up and went downstairs to see what he was doing. He was standing naked in the kitchen with the eiderdown around his feet and hanging the clock on a nail in the west wall, he pulled the weights on each chain to wind the clock and stood still until they could hear the ticking above the wind, which was now subsiding. The hands showed a quarter to nine, but it was night. He turned and seemed to be asking what time he should set it to. Ingrid said to leave it as it was. Then they went upstairs again, and no-one came.

## 10

There are many ways to row a boat, and he didn't know any of them. He flailed irritably with the oars in the tholepins and wrestled with the wrist straps while Ingrid sat on a sheepskin in the stern laughing at him. She explained things to him and pointed out skerries and islands only just visible in the darkness. He tried to do better and wanted praise, like a child, and she gave him praise, thinking he was a child, and that he was getting more and more handsome by the day, and that it was unbearable.

She told him to row over the sound in the direction of Gjesøya, then south on the seaward side, where the swell was becoming increasingly heavy. His fingers were too short and he thrashed the oars against the breakers. They changed places and Ingrid took them around the island and into a gap in the rock face, where there was a natural harbour, moored the boat to a driftwood log and said there was something she wanted to show him.

They waded up through squeaking, snow-covered seaweed into the hollow, where the Barrøyers had once broken new ground and came to a haybarn they called the pavilion. Ingrid opened the door and told him to go in. They sat on some old, dusty hay listening to the sea. She said the weather would calm down before long, and sooner or later someone would be coming to Barrøy, so this would be his hideaway, words he understood, this is a different island, she said, they will have dogs with them, and he understood that, too.

They listened to the sea.

He laid a hand on her thigh, and began to talk in a new voice, it sounded like confidences, or warnings; he became excited and gesticulated, squeezed her and wanted to illustrate something or other, and Ingrid was pleased she didn't have the language to ask him how old he was.

She clasped his mutilated hand and held it to her face and let him speak. Now it sounded more like he was trying to persuade her, which again she was pleased she didn't understand, he was beginning to regain his strength, to rediscover something he had forgotten, something he thought was lost, and a new weariness began to make its presence felt, the beginning of a darkness she knew she could not bear, a life without him.

She forced him to row on the way back and sat in such a way that she could cry without him seeing. He saw nonetheless, drew in the oars and sat motionless. Then he placed a hand on each of her shoulders. She rested her cheek on the mittens, but without turning her head. She didn't say anything, either. They drifted. Then he carried on rowing.

*

Next evening they went out again. She taught him how to use a hand line, how to hold a fish, cut its throat and gut it, forced him out into the heavy swell on the seaward side and showed him that wet mittens are warm, and how a rowing boat can be thrown into the breakers, but be sucked out again after a bit of magic with the oars. She said it was up to him whether he froze or was injured, and now his hair was a thick, jet-black mat in which she could bury her fingers. And that night she couldn't sleep, he could, his breathing was as peaceful and regular as Nelly's, and that made her even more afraid.

She got up and looked out: the sea was as smooth as oil in all directions.

She started packing eiderdowns, rugs and clothes, filled the food chest as if she were kitting a man out for a fishing season in Lofoten, woke him and told him to get dressed, in a whisper.

He looked at her in puzzlement.

She rowed them south through the sound and into the gap on Gjesøya. They walked up to the barn and lay together in the hay until the sun was high in the sky, and she said she would return every evening, with food and water, and herself, and took her leave. He held her back, they lay down in the hay and took their leave of one another, and when she finally rowed away she had never been a tinier stump of driftwood in the sea.

Back at the house on Barrøy she set about erasing his traces and tracks, and hers. She looked in the mirror and smeared soot on her face, went from one window to the next, peering north and east, nobody was coming.

She felt stupid and washed her face, tidied up and played with Koshka the cat, and now she couldn't sleep in the North Chamber. She fetched the telescope from the quay house and lay in her parents' bed in the South Chamber staring at Gjesøya, through the treacherous telescope without seeing anything at all, and she didn't shut an eye until the night made her blind.

When next morning too the islands resembled specks of rust on a shiny mirror, she felt even more stupid and rowed south and took him out in the boat so the waves could make him seasick and they had something to laugh at. She set him ashore again, they waited until he had regained his balance, then they went out again. They fished and gutted the catch, she left him on the island and rowed home, turned and rowed back, mooring the boat to the log, and lay with him in the barn until darkness fell. And even though the new wind was no more than a light breeze, she decided that the sea was too rough and stayed there until yet another day dawned, before rowing home in thick snow and sleet and arriving for the second time in a cold house which she had to spend the rest of the day making habitable, fortunately it cost her all her reserves of energy.

She wound up the clock and adjusted the hands, played with the cat, made some food, and wanted to card and spin, but she wasn't able to.

She lay in the South Chamber with the telescope and watched the day wane over Gjesøya, grey sea, the occasional flutter of birds, until they, too, passed out of sight.

She got up again, dressed, walked around the island in a snow shower and found nothing and went home again, intending to make some coffee. She stumbled on the even floor, got to her feet again and slumped into the rocking chair, fell asleep and dreamed of a pine cone she had drawn at school as a child. She woke up, feeling refreshed, her skin twitching as if someone had blown on her, went up to the loft and got out her old sketch pad and crayons, remembering the teacher who had once, with a triumphant expression, placed a huge pine cone on the desk and told the children to draw it, a gigantic seed vessel, the like of which none of them had ever seen. Ingrid's cone came to resemble the shell of a snail, which the teacher laughed at. But then all of the children's cones resembled snail shells, conches or seashells, to a greater or lesser degree, and Ingrid went up to bed determined to have him write something before he left her – for he would be leaving, he had to, that was the whole point – whether she could read what he wrote or not, one day she would understand.

# 11

They were at that time of the year when everything living dies, when man and beast shrink into themselves and become even smaller than they already are, when nature is void of any sound but the sea, and no prayer has the power to arouse anything at all.

Ingrid had taken the tattered clothes down from the drying rack and piled them on the fish crates in the boat shed, and now she found herself holding another handful of wood shavings, the difference between frostbite and warmth, summer and winter, life and death, when she heard the throb of an engine, which wasn't her own heart, and she fell into an inner calm that she thought had abandoned her for good.

She went up to the house, tousled her hair, smeared fresh soot on her face, pulled an extra scarf over her head and went out with the peat bin and watched as the trading post's old cargo boat rounded the headland and came alongside the new quay.

She let go of the peat bin and walked calmly down, her eyes scanning the snow for tracks, she found none, continued to the water's edge and saw the boiled-egg officer standing at the rail looking up at her. The skipper threw the mooring ropes ashore. Ingrid slipped the loops over the bollards. Behind the officer stood four uniformed soldiers, and behind them the local lensmann, Police Chief Henriksen, who hadn't been much of a man before the war and whose participation in it hadn't made him any more of one, no dogs though.

The officer stepped onto the quay, folded his begloved hands in front of his stomach and shivered, the red scar across the bridge of his nose turned redder, his good-natured eyes were no less so now, he said his name was Hargel, Leutnant Hargel, and began to pace to and fro while Ingrid opened the doors of the quay house and let the winter light in on the bodies. He peered in and said "*Mein Gott*", turned and shouted something to the soldiers, who clambered ashore one after the other, wearing face masks and with two stretchers, and started carrying out the earthly remains of the dead.

Ingrid showed them how to work the windlass.

They lowered the bodies into the boat and laid them on pallets in the hold and on the deck, and sprinkled them with a white powder. Then they hoisted an iron tank onto land, containing the same powder, and also covered the quay-house floor, then the quay and the windlass, so it looked as if a whiter snow had covered the old.

The officer said something, which Ingrid construed as her having to wait for a few days before hosing it down, and he demonstrated the process using his begloved hands and making hissing sounds. She noticed that the shot-damaged roof was dripping and knew she would have to wait until the spring, until the summer, if indeed she ever went in there again, turned to Henriksen and told him about the body in the barn loft.

He, the officer and two soldiers went up with her.

Ingrid had covered him with the uniform and the horse cloth. Hargel asked for a light. Ingrid unbolted and opened the hatch through which they used to pitch hay. The soldiers pulled out the corpse and were about to examine it. Hargel pushed them aside and went down on one knee like a doctor. Ingrid looked away and heard words like *Frost, ertrunken, Gewalt* . . . Henriksen asked if she had found him *here*.

"Yes."

"He must have been alive to get here then?"

"Yes," Ingrid said, but he was dead when she found him.

He asked why she hadn't notified them.

She said she had and turned to Hargel, who had got to his feet, and said in Norwegian that she didn't think the man was German as he was wearing the same rags as the others, the uniform was only spread over him, like a blanket.

The Lensmann translated and Hargel pulled her into the light, scrutinised her and said something that only became threatening as Henriksen translated.

He wasn't *wearing* the uniform, she repeated.

"Why didn't you report it?" Henriksen repeated.

Ingrid asked him if he was "hard o' hearen'".

Henriksen went red in the face, and Hargel looked with

interest at each of them in turn. With the same remarkable composure, Ingrid replied that the weather had made it impossible for her to report it earlier.

The soldiers laid the dead man on the stretcher and carried him out. The others went down to the yard, Hargel still holding the uniform, he wasn't finished with it, turned out the pockets and found some paper that had disintegrated, showed an interest in the military insignia, held up a pair of spectacles with only one lens and peered through it.

She asked them if they wanted some coffee.

Hargel said, gruffly, no and asked her if she knew what rank this officer had held.

"No."

Hadn't she noticed that he was a colonel?

"No."

He said something else, and Henriksen asked what she was answering "no" to.

Ingrid said she knew nothing about German ranks.

Hargel appeared to be at a loss and asked if she had any weapons.

Ingrid nodded and went in to fetch the Krag rifle, the harpoon gun and the shotgun. Hargel examined them and said the possession of weapons was illegal and passed them to the soldier who had come back from the boat.

Ingrid said they'd always had weapons, they shot eagles, porpoises, mink . . .

Hargel asked if she knew how to use them.

"Yes."

"That one, too?" he said, pointing to the harpoon gun.

"Yes."

He shook his head and said something to Henriksen, who ordered her to fetch any ammunition she might have.

"Enough for a whole war," the Lensmann translated when she returned with the two boxes and the harpoons.

There then followed a lengthy discussion in German, and Ingrid was struck by how old Henriksen seemed, stooped, breathing heavily and hawking, a pale shadow of the authority he had once been, she wondered whether there was any particular reason for this.

Hargel went over to her, removed his glove and spat on a stumpy finger, ran it down her cheek and examined the soot.

"*Die Frauen haben Angst*," he mumbled philosophically, women are frightened, and wiped his finger on the uniform. "*Eine Beleidigung*." An insult.

He resumed his discussion with Henriksen, and Ingrid heard words like *Feuer* and *Radio* and burst out that she didn't have a radio, and waited as if standing to attention, until Hargel asked her another question, did she live here on her own?

Yes, her aunt was in hospital and the menfolk in Lofoten.

"So there's just you?"

"Yes."

"What do you live off?" he said, gazing south and addressing himself to the snow-covered gardens.

Ingrid didn't understand the question.

He asked if they had lived here throughout the war.

Ingrid said they had always lived here.

His eyes leisurely scanned the buildings and he said something about "*schreckliche Armut*". Terrible poverty.

Henriksen smirked.

Ingrid said she wanted to show him something in the boat shed and they accompanied her down to the waterside, the pile of clothes, she supposed they would want to take them as well?

"They're P.O.W. uniforms," the Lensmann said.

Ingrid listened.

Hargel asked where she had found them.

She told them where she had found every single garment, but when this was translated, it met with no interest. Hargel went out again and walked along the shore to the quay, remembered something, turned and shouted. Lensmann Henriksen turned to Ingrid and said she could keep the harpoon gun, but they would have to take the Krag and the shotgun with them, and the ammunition.

Ingrid nodded and asked if there had only been P.O.W.s on the ship. Henriksen asked if she was stupid or what. The soldier came up and gave her two pieces of paper, one the *Verordnung für Zivilisten in der Besatzungszone*, regulations for civilians in occupied territory . . . she hadn't seen the other one before. She folded them and accompanied the men to the quay, was about to lift the ropes off the bollards, but was stopped by a *Warte mal.* Hargel was standing amidst the bodies on the deck and called up to her:

"*Haben Sie keine Tiere*?" Haven't you got any livestock?

"*Nein.*"

He nodded.

"*Und wie viele Boote?*" And how many boats?

"Four," Ingrid said.

He nodded again and signalled with a finger. She lifted the loops and stood at attention as before, until they had backed out of the sound and set a course for the village, she wondered why she hadn't moved the body in the barn down to the quay house with the others and burned the uniform, why they hadn't asked whether she had found a boat, or searched for one, no-one makes it here alive without a boat. She reflected on the conversation and the tracks in the snow she still couldn't find and wondered whether she had heard *Gewalt*, force, or *keine Gewalt*, no force, or *ertrunken*, drowned, or *nicht ertrunken*, not drowned, and eventually decided that whatever they had said or she had understood, they would be back, it had something to do with a feeling she had about Henriksen.

That evening she didn't dare go to Gjesøya, the sea was too calm and the darkness too light. She lay in the South Chamber with the telescope scanning the islands, thinking now nothing is visible, now I can row, but she stayed put, for she was asleep.

# 12

They had left behind the tank of white powder. Ingrid filled a bucket and sprinkled it over the hayloft floor. When the tide was almost out she walked over to Karvika and began to stare into the sea where the boat had sunk. She couldn't see anything, she waited until the tide was at its lowest, and still she couldn't see anything.

But today it was too light to row and it remained so.

She dragged the rags from the boat shed to the Nordnes headland, burned them and disposed of the ashes in the sea. The change in the weather failed to materialise. Binoculars were being trained on her. Someone was watching her. When dusk fell she nonetheless set out in the boat and rowed at breakneck speed to Gjesøya, sheltered by Barrøy, moored the boat in the gap in the rock face and ran up the grass slope, where she stumbled upon two sets of tracks, thin crusts of ice in dark, wet holes staring up at her – both led from the barn and northwards across the fields, one clearly footprints, the other a trail of drag marks. She followed them, walking north, running, until she realised he had panicked and tried to swim for it, but hadn't been able to, yet had still survived.

She turned on her heel, ran back and tore open the door.

He seemed to be asleep, but he didn't wake when she shook him, he was soaked to the skin, his clothes were flecked with ice. She heard breathing, gurgling, and recognised the signs of fever, he said something and writhed, brandished an arm, but didn't open his eyes.

Ingrid screamed, rolled him off the rug and placed it outside on the snow, pulled him out by his feet onto the rug, threw the eiderdown over him, dragged him down through the gap in the rocks, but couldn't get him up into the boat. She rolled him off the rug again, put it and the eiderdown in the stern and raised him into a sitting position, locked her arms behind his back and stood up and fell with him into the boat, hitting the back of her head in the process.

She covered him with the eiderdown and rowed home through an ocean of time and moored near the Swedes' quay house, manoeuvred him out of the boat and managed to drag him up to the house before she passed out.

When she came to, he was looking down at her. She remembered that this had happened to her before. She felt hot, dangerously hot. He muttered something, his wet eyes looked as though they were about to be extinguished.

Ingrid struggled to her feet, took off his clothes and mercilessly rubbed him down, something eerie arose from his exhausted body. She went up to the loft and fetched the sketch pad and crayon, pressed them into his hands, massaged him with her palms and pummelled him with her fists, called him an idiot who couldn't wait, an impatient child who didn't trust her . . . She ran upstairs again and fetched another eiderdown, continued to rub and pummel him until she herself was spent, and she was found there three days later.

# II

# 1

Ingrid knew as soon as she opened her eyes in the white room that she would have to go back to Barrøy to regain her senses. To find the man again. To salvage her childhood and life, everything that was on Barrøy, an empty, deserted island in the sea, and yet the idea seemed so alien that some outsider must have weasled it into her mind.

It wasn't the first time she had opened her eyes in the white room, she had done that a week ago and stood at the window gazing across the snow-covered ground that resembled a freshly ironed sheet, wreathed by trees standing like soldiers in formation, with a perfectly conical spruce in the centre, it was like a black tooth, as it stood there waiting to be decorated because it was Christmas, inside and outside the hospital.

She had spoken to doctors, nurses and an old man who came into her room every day to do the cleaning, which he found shameful and only did because his wife was ill and they needed the money, he said. And he always sat in the chair looking out at the same spruce tree and told her he didn't mind doing women's work as the nutcases in this place were nicer than his workmates down at the harbour – they had it in for him because he was too old to carry a sack of coffee beans from the belly of a ship up the wobbly plank into the warehouse, that was before he fell.

Ingrid knew she wasn't mad when she realised that *he* was, even though she too was a patient, like him. He was decrepit, stooped and almost hairless, and he didn't come to do the cleaning but to hide, and he had chosen Ingrid.

She got out of bed and wanted to lay a hand on his shoulder, as he had these enormous hands, like her grandfather's. But the sound of the sea wouldn't go away, it would never be pure again, the lightning flashed behind her eyelids, but by then he had already managed to grip her fingertips, to hold them, the way a child holds an adult's hand, it felt both disgusting and good, he was human and she could trust him.

Ingrid opened her eyes in the white room and remembered they had said she was dehydrated, she hadn't known what that meant, and that she was weak from hunger and had been beaten black and blue and had suffered something she ought to forget, though there was still a risk of it returning, so she had to learn to deal with it, here in the hospital they couldn't decide whether forgetting and remembering were two sides of the same coin, that was why she was here.

She was given food and medicine, she pinched rubber tubes, blinked when they asked if she understood what they said, recited the names of her parents and grandparents, said "ow" when they stuck needles in her and nodded when they hit her below the kneecap with small rubber hammers . . . From the window she could see an electric cable winding like a black snake through the snow from the building where she was to the conical spruce tree, where she was able to count twenty-three dots of light on a grey winter's day, the only Christmas tree in the town with electric lighting, and at the top shone a star, which suddenly went out.

They said she had to eat more, and she did.

They told her to walk along the corridors and lift her knees because she wasn't an old woman and there was no reason to shuffle around like one. She went up and down the stairs and talked to people she recognised from day to day and froze in her thin shift. She found her way back to the room without any help and lay down and slept and was visited by the old man, who wanted to sit with her, pensive and silent as a mummy.

"Look!" he said suddenly, his head turned to the window. "Now it's all going to cock!"

He got up, ran out howling and was down the corridor like a bat out of hell. Ingrid crept out of bed, slipped her feet into thick knitted socks and from the window she could see two men carrying a ladder through the snow and propping it against the tree, one stood supporting it while the other climbed up and changed a light bulb in the star, which – when it was lit – made the ladder and the two men look like a character from some foreign alphabet, and fear was pumped through her as if by a piston.

*

She told the doctor she didn't want the old man in her room anymore, he reminded her of her grandfather. The doctor said he was harmless, to himself and to her.

"He frightens me."

"Why's that?"

"He's dead."

The doctor asked when her grandfather had died and how.

Ingrid told him, and he sat nodding until her voice dissolved into a mishmash of sound, and the unease disappeared, he could see that in her face, could *she* see into his, there was no more to it than that.

But then he didn't get up and leave her, as he usually did in such moments of clarity, but sat squirming, embarrassed, because, he said, he had something to confess.

Ingrid gazed at him with interest.

He hadn't believed her story about the bodies, no-one had heard about a boat sinking, so he thought it could have been a delusion, or what he called a psychosis, at best a nightmare, but yesterday he had been flicking through some old newspapers and found this, reported by N.T.B.

He picked up a page he had torn out and placed it in her lap. Ingrid read: "German survivors shot at by British pilots near Rosøy on 27th November . . . A German steamer named M.S. *Rigel* sank and survivors say British pilots strafed the lifeboats and those who had made it ashore . . . This proves how British pilots systematically shoot at survivors of sinking German ships."

The news item was no more than six or seven centimetres long and three wide, dated December 7, which was three weeks ago, and there wasn't a word about how many people had died, nor about any Russians, Ingrid had talked about Russians, hadn't she?

She imagined the currents in the sea and the winds and all the islands and skerries between the islands of Rosøy and Barrøy.

"That's a long way, miles and miles . . ."

"What?"

She didn't answer.

This is the only report there is, he said, he had searched everywhere, but thought nonetheless that it was likely those things she had seen and experienced were what he termed realities.

Ingrid stared at him.

He asked if she had understood.

She asked whether she had been alone when she was found.

He said yes, but seemed unsure and appeared to be concerned that she had fallen into a reverie again. And she was going to ask how many boats there had been on Barrøy when they found her, but realised he was no islander. Then he told her without prompting that her medical record said a certain Lensmann Henriksen and a Leutnant Hargel had found her during a routine assignment.

She asked to see the case papers.

He said no and sat drumming his fingers on the file, looking out at the Christmas tree, where once again twenty-three lights and one star shone, whereupon he opened the file anyway, mumbling that she could read it if she wanted, there was nothing wrong with her, unlike her mother, he had treated her, too; on the contrary, all the evidence suggested now that Ingrid had been traumatised by war, like so many others, those who had been evacuated from Finnmark, for example, where the Germans had carried out a scorched earth campaign; refugees were streaming south in boat after boat, he'd already had lots of them here and really wished war could be stated as a diagnosis, then there would be a kind of truth in his files.

Ingrid read that Leutnant Hargel's first names were Albert Emil and she knew that he had encroached upon her life in ways very different from simply confiscating her weapons and removing dead bodies, but not how. She also realised she had told the doctor about Russians, but was unsure whether she had talked about *her* Russian; she asked what physical state she had been in when she arrived, and had to repeat the question, whereupon he muttered:

"Pretty bruised, after a fall maybe, down a flight of stairs?"

The sea would never be pure again, but the searing flashes were gone, and the foreign letters of the alphabet, and she had no pain. She was allowed to keep the newspaper cutting and clung to it as if it were a lifebuoy, even though it spoke of German troops with no mention of any Russians. But she had heard about it from Henriksen when they came to fetch the bodies, though that didn't make it any more credible, and she had found P.O.W. uniforms, balls of wood shavings used for warmth, men with no names or faces, except for one, and perhaps *it* too was a notion that came from the outside, unless she was carrying it within herself, his face; now she could visualise it again, but that was all.

# 2

They said she was strong and showing signs of improvement, they also seemed to mean it, both the staff and her fellow patients, the latter thought she was employed there.

The doctor who never smiled continued to offer her friendly counsel, and began to call her a remarkable woman, a choice of words Ingrid asked him to clarify. He looked embarrassed and mumbled some vague explanation, so she chose to focus mainly on the "woman" part, which made her smile, and she wasn't used to that, so she checked herself and bowed her head in a kind of bashfulness, unless this behaviour had been sparked by some memory, a hazy shadow, or was it only to pick up the pencil that had fallen out of her hand at the onset of the smile?

He asked her what she was writing.

Ingrid was writing a letter and wanted to give it to him. He shook his head and said she would soon be returning to a life the hospital had no part in, then he took it all the same; it was for Suzanne, who had once been like a daughter to Ingrid, but she, too, had left her.

He asked her for the pencil.

She gave it to him.

He made some changes to the letter, finished reading it and said, still without smiling, that Ingrid was being too hard on people she liked and told her she had made some grammatical and spelling mistakes, which he had taken the liberty of correcting.

Ingrid smiled and said she hadn't made any mistakes, not since her schooldays. He grabbed the letter again, looked at it and, after a few grunts of acknowledgement, repeated that she was a remarkable woman, before adding – as she rubbed out his amendments and folded the letter – that she was intelligent, but of the more intuitive rather than the reflective type, and he found that confusing.

Ingrid laughed and asked if he was sure it wasn't him who was mad.

He still didn't laugh, but he made no move to leave, there was something else he wanted to discuss with her: he had received some money which she was to have, and a letter from her parish priest, a certain Johannes Malmberget. He hadn't wanted to give it to her before for fear of confusing her on top of everything else that was going on, apparently this priest had borrowed money from her father, you see, and was now entreating forgiveness for having hoped for so many years after her father's death that nobody would remember, now he wanted to pay his dues, the letter said.

The doctor said he considered this invidious.

"Invidious?"

He explained what "invidious" meant and Ingrid closed her eyes. The old rural parish priest who disappeared when war broke out, with his young wife and two adolescent children, a mysterious, shadowy figure, who'd had an impact on Ingrid's life before, in a crucial way. Now she saw him disappearing again, as before, and said she needed to know how many had gone down with the ship.

"You keep changing the subject," the doctor said. "Which ship?"

"The *Rigel.*"

"I see, no, they never publish the casualty figures."

This, by the way, was one of those things she should cast from her mind.

He got to his feet, stood with one hand on the bedhead and repeated that she shouldn't be so hard on Suzanne in the letter if she wanted her to come back. In addition, she should allow old Ingvaldsen to sit here, *she* might be leaving, but the old man was going nowhere, he would never be able to remember anything either, and a good job, too.

Ingrid asked what had happened to him.

"Ask him," the doctor said.

Ingrid eyed him. He said:

"He lost his wife and three sons when the town was bombed, and a brother. He dug them out of the ruins with his own hands. He's been here ever since."

Ingrid considered this an explanation of a kind, but there had to be more, not because it wasn't enough, but because there must always be more, otherwise there is nothing, and she wasn't able to put this into words, no matter how clear it was to her, these shadows that rose and sank inside her. She thanked him for telling her, the old man could sit here and be like her grandfather, with the same enormous hands, hands that could never leave her.

Ingrid opened her eyes in the white room, and from the window saw the twenty-three lights and the star on the tree being sucked up into a black day – only to be extinguished completely, so slowly that she became unsure whether they really had gone, she could still see them, it was now January.

The rain lashed against the windowpanes, the snow vanished, an incessant howl resounded in the ventilation shafts. She crept out of bed and was on her tiptoes trying to close the hatch when the door opened, and in walked Ingvaldsen with a plaster on his shaven pate. He took a seat in the chair by the window and looked out at the lights that were no longer there. Ingrid went over and tore off the plaster, saying he didn't need it, he didn't have any wounds, it was his mind that was muddled, his nerves. He smiled archly and said he knew that, but they still didn't say no when he asked for the plaster, bless them.

Ingrid stuck the plaster back on his head and asked whether she had put it on right.

"Yah, yah," he said after checking with his fingertips, whereupon he pressed his face against the glass again, his hands down by his sides, and gaped out at the rain.

"There's nothing to see," Ingrid said.

"Yes, there is," he said. "I can see something."

"What?"

"Have a look yourself."

Ingrid turned her back on him, sat on the edge of the bed and arched backwards so the upper part of her body bent towards the floor on the other side, reached out with her right arm and pulled the string as she swung up again, remaining in the same inclined position until the door opened and one of the carers came in, her name was Eva Sofie. In a voice that took even her by surprise, Ingrid asked if they could have some coffee.

"This isn't a restaurant," Eva Sofie said sourly, and was about to go again. But then she spotted the tray with the remains of the breakfast on the bedside table, went over to fetch it and on her way out told Ingrid to go to the duty room herself and ask for some coffee.

Ingrid thanked her, still without getting up, and in the same strange voice said it was the seventh of January. Eva Sofie stopped and gave a sulky smile, went over to the noticeboard by the window, balanced the tray on the fingertips of her left hand, marked a cross on a chart detailing days and hours and things Ingrid had to remember, and not forget, the life that told her not only who she had been, but also who she was, so that she could live with herself, it looked like a completed crossword.

Eva Sofie mumbled O.K., O.K., and fine, let go of the pencil, which was left dangling from the string, and went out with Ingrid hot on her heels.

Ingrid was given two cups of coffee in the duty room, she chatted amiably with the four staff members sitting there, she knew them by name, and was almost dancing as she skipped along the corridor, a cup in each hand, backed against door number 27, thrust it open with her bottom and a second later saw a red flash on the wall in front of her, in the corridor, and was flung into the same wall by a violent blast and a storm of broken glass.

# 3

Ingrid opened her eyes in a new and equally white room, but now she was lying on her stomach and had pains in her back and head from the shards of glass they had plucked from her with tweezers. Then they had patched her up with lots of small, black cross-stitches which she could see in two mirrors they held up for her, but it was the same doctor.

He asked if she could hear him, she blinked yes.

He went through one elaborate detail after the other, which Ingrid still remembered so vividly that it was almost intolerable, and only then did he tell her that a snowplough had driven over an unexploded shell left from the time bombs rained down on the town. One wing of the hospital had been obliterated, two people killed and eleven injured.

Ingrid shouted into her pillow.

"It wasn't snowing!"

He sat in a chair directly in front of her, when he lifted his head she could see him. He said quietly, as if to a child, with a rare tone of respect in his voice, that they weren't clearing snow, they were moving the plough, the cuts to her head and back would heal.

She buried her face in the starched, white linen, the blessed and the pure, and enquired after Ingvaldsen, from the doctor's silence she realised the old man was one of the dead and she closed her eyes again.

The chair came closer and his hands held her head and forced it up again.

He searched her eyes while *she* searched his, knowing without needing to ask that his name was Falc Johannesen, though he preferred to be called Falc, Erik Falc, because he had a brother, also a doctor, with whom he did not want to be confused under any circumstances, he had confided this to her once when his face almost broke into a smile, because his brother had turned into a German.

Then he mumbled that from now on she would remember more.

She was about to protest – but woke up on the floor by the kitchen bench on Barrøy and saw his hand dangling down towards her face in order to touch it – as if in supplication.

She took it and stood up, feeling a taut, distant sensation in every cell, and they went upstairs together and lay beside each other in the North Chamber listening to each other's breathing. They fell asleep and woke and the fever was gone, but they stayed where they were, and there was no more to be said, no confidences or attempts at persuasion, no prayers, they were a silent, tight-lipped communion on this, the penultimate day.

She got up and cooked, they ate and lay together and slept.

She asked why he hadn't been content to stay in the haybarn on Gjesøya. But their bodies were warm and they lay beside each other for hour after hour and knew what had to happen. He slipped out of bed, dressed, went downstairs, cooked and called through the vent in the floor for her to get up and dress, there was no mistaking his intention.

She did so slowly in order not to miss out on a single movement, the way she dressed, buttoning a button, tying a ribbon, throwing her hair forwards and dividing it into three streams that could be plaited with fingers that know their way around in the dark, she kissed the tuft at the end, which looked like a besom, and tossed it over her shoulder with a flourish that was hers alone.

When she went downstairs, he was sitting staring at the papers the soldier had given her when they confiscated the weapons, he seemed to understand what he was reading and stopped when she appeared.

She asked again:

"*Deutsch?*"

He shook his head – a Russian who has some knowledge of German in a German-occupied territory is far more likely than a German who has some knowledge of Russian in the same country, she said this aloud and again he seemed to understand every word.

After they had eaten and Ingrid wanted to do more of what was her or to be as she had once been, he held her back and said

Leningrad and academy and engineer, he had said this before, now it etched itself into her like a belief and a conviction. She sat down and placed her school sketch pad between them, depicting fir cones that looked like shells, flowers, boats and mountains, and he wrote the number 22, it could have been his age or his year of birth, it didn't make any difference, and even if their ways were soon to part, she asked him to write more.

He took the pencil in his left hand and held it like a poised dart, placed the point on the paper and wrote letters she could neither decipher nor pronounce, a single slow line, then one more, the way you write your mother tongue, it struck her, and he put down the pencil underneath, as if drawing a line underneath everything, unless it was to cross it all out.

She turned round the pad and noticed that every line began with the same symbols, in the same order, he had written three paragraphs each containing three short lines, one beneath the other, they not only looked similar, they were identical, she asked him what they meant.

He laughed and pushed the pad aside.

Ingrid sat watching him until she had to turn her face to the window. She said there was a light cloud covering, and the sea was as smooth as a mirror, *that* was the signal, not the way he had put down his pencil, and he understood.

They went to the loft and lay beside each other without moving.

They got up and dressed one another, the rucksack was packed, she had given him all the money and ration coupons she had, as well as a knife and a compass. She had explained that he had to take account of drift, read the direction and rhythm of the waves, four or five hours to the mainland, now that he had learned how to row and sail, tonight there was so little wind he would have to row.

She also said she had taught him all this in the hope that he would have the wits to disappear while she was asleep, but that it was good he hadn't understood or chosen not to. She wrote something on the pad, tore out the sheet, folded it and put it in the pocket of her father's fishing smock he was wearing, which made him look like an old salt; on it she had written what was necessary for him to get help from kind folk, who would understand, so he could cross a country and a continent on foot and one day arrive at his childhood home and show his mother that he was alive, all the things he should have done of his own accord: steal her money and one of the boats and disappear while she was asleep because she couldn't do this, say goodbye.

He couldn't do this, either – so now they walk out into the silence together and down to the boat shed and push out the færing, his smile is a white wedge in the night; on an island time contracts and stands still, they have no words, the færing is afloat, the full moon is enormous and again she has to point out the cleft in the rugged mainland ridge, just visible beneath Cassiopeia's electrified barbed wire before it fades into grey down, how many degrees on the compass, the currents, the waves that change direction close to the shore.

He nods.

It is impossible to hold each other, he goes on board and sits on the thwart, an oar in each mutilated hand, ties the straps she has taught him to use around his wrists and starts rowing, rests on the oars and shouts something, carries on rowing. Ingrid has no voice and is invisible, the wind has coiled up inside a snail shell and stays there all night, nothing is happening and nothing has happened.

The doctor who hates his own good name has seen tears before, he hasn't seen much else since he passed his exams in Misery, how long ago was that? He has lost count of the years, even a doctor has both to remember and forget, so he stays in the chair, more or less, during the time it takes for Ingrid to be able to see him through dry eyes, she who thought they had run dry ages ago.

She says she wished it had been her and not Ingvaldsen sitting at the window when the shell exploded, on the day without snow.

Erik Falc doesn't believe in fairy tales or God or Providence, he says, but she has to take this as a sign that she is alive and will continue to be, no-one lives without meaning, there is a meaning in just being alive, he manages to intone, or words to this effect. And she thinks it was well expressed, but also utterly meaningless, so she looks at him with a contempt that is foreign to her, and asks in a voice that isn't hers either – and which she can't stand the sound of – whether she had been trying to take her own life when they found her on the island, Lensmann

Henriksen and that officer, what was his name, Hargel?

Erik Falc looks at her in surprise and says he doesn't know, but – actually, he says – it wouldn't surprise him.

She asks what wouldn't surprise him.

That she had been trying to commit suicide.

She asks what that was supposed to mean.

"You're playing with me," he says.

"No, I'm not," she says.

"But you won't try again," he declares, making it sound more like a guarantee than an idle hope, and Ingrid asks if this means the two men saved her life?

He says he doesn't know that either and she can finally ask the all-important question: Did they find her sketch pad on the kitchen table?

Now he is completely nonplussed.

Ingrid closes her eyes and hauls in those dark days: she has a rough outline of when she came to the hospital up to the present day, the intricate crossword on the wall in the old room, she knows it off by heart, the days' empty numbers, but she can't remember if she managed to hide the pad with the Russian writing, three verses of three lines each, it is somewhere in the two or three days that still remain dark.

She counts the days again and they are and remain gone. So they must be on Barrøy, she has to go back and search for them. And Erik Falc, the doctor, says that is precisely what they have been talking about the whole time. Ingrid tries to heave a sigh of relief or to prepare herself for something that is about to happen, but then he asks why she didn't go with him, the Russian, when he left the island, and help him.

She feels a spider's web on her face and says that then they would have found Barrøy empty and become suspicious.

He says that cannot be the reason.

She looks down and says no, and that is the worst of it.

"You didn't trust him?"

"No, I didn't," Ingrid says, feeling that now she can hide again, that she still doesn't know the difference between what has to be remembered and what forgotten.

He places a hand on her shoulder, fixes her with a long gaze and goes out, returning before the duty shift changes and says:

"They're taking out the stitches tomorrow. You can leave on Friday. I've arranged for you to go on a refugee boat."

# 4

Eva Sofie takes out the stitches and, using two mirrors, allows Ingrid to see her own back, small pink crosses over white skin and her shaven head which, together, they manage to conceal beneath a new plait, or two, which they tie together, and Eva Sofie says that Ingrid should start wearing a brassiere, at any rate when men are present, such as on this trip south, she has seen these boats, they're not nice places to be.

It is her daily duties in the shower room that have put this idea into Eva Sofie's head. Every morning Ingrid and two elderly women from the same ward, Ada and Signy, both with long, grey hair like straw, are led three floors down and have to undress in a cold, white changing room with echoing walls and then stand between some serpentine steel pipes in a tiled room and be rinsed down from all directions with water that is too hot. It also comes from above, like rain. Eva Sofie calls it a shower, and says how important it is for them to stay there for four minutes, gyrating like ballet dancers, even though the water comes from all sides and they could just as well have stood still, whilst Eva Sofie rests her hands on a red and a blue tap, controlling the flow of water like a driver with two steering wheels, and checks that they do what they have been told with regard to soap and rinsing, and groin and armpits and hair, and that afterwards they dry themselves on rough, newly washed towels, which make their skin burn and become nubbly. Ada and Signy are more self-conscious than Ingrid, and that helps, they get accustomed to neither the changing room nor the cold water, but they are in here together and giggle and laugh like schoolgirls.

And Ingrid, who used to think she was a clean person, now she hasn't been aware of the smell of her own body since her island was struck by death; the spurting jets of water caress and prickle her skin and inspire her to stretch her arms above her head and spread her fingers into the metallic chandelier releasing the shower of water like a cloud; she spins around and performs more pirouettes than Eva Sofie cares to see, so she wrenches hard at the red tap, causing Ingrid to rush out of the ice-cold water with a howl, which is not without an element of pleasure, the four minutes are now up.

It is here in the shower that Eva Sofie has noticed that Ingrid's breasts are larger than her own.

Ingrid has no real objection to the suggestion regarding the brassiere, even though there has always been a lack of confidentiality between them, as Eva Sofie regards the war as a personal insult and can't stop herself telling people that she is the one who has suffered the greatest losses, both a boyfriend and a secretarial career have gone up in smoke as a result of this hell on earth. And everyone can visualise the man Eva Sofie lost on the northern front in the first phase of the war, because she walks around with a photograph of him in the breast pocket of her uniform, next to a watch and a pencil with bite-marks and lipstick on the end, and shows the picture to both those who want to see it and those who have already seen it: a grainy photograph of a young man so far away in a field that he could laugh and cry and no-one would be any the wiser. He was ten years older than Eva Sofie, while Eva Sofie is one year older than Ingrid, and she has no children, come to mention it – she does so herself all the time – to make a point of another personal tragedy caused by the war.

When Eva Sofie is not on duty, which as a rule she is, she spends her time at home baking, in a house that has been partially reconstructed after the bombing, using sifted wheat flour, sugar and a few small chopped nuts that she gets from the hospital kitchen, or steals, and she takes the cakes to work and shares them around, with a face as if she is giving injections. The patients like and fear her in equal measure, while the staff are used to her. And the cakes are good, they are sweet, with these nuts and coarse sugar that resembles scorched ice crystals.

This time she brought the bra with stays, which turned out to be too tight, tight enough for Eva Sofie's assessment of the difference in their respective sizes to be proved correct, yet too tight for Ingrid to put it on at first, as the wounds on her back were still painful; they packed it away in a small, blue suitcase, which Eva Sofie had also brought from home, with brass fittings on all eight corners, plus a light-brown corset.

She also gave her a greyish-white frieze jacket of the type the patients had to drape over themselves when they were led from one wing to another, and some pinafores, which Ingrid didn't think she would have any use for, but accepted all the same, and a jumper, four pairs of socks, five headscarves, a sou'wester and some underwear, which Eva Sofie said she didn't need any more, even though it looked brand new, and she cried when Ingrid dressed on Friday morning and appeared wearing an outfit of ordinary clothes, which neither she herself nor the others thought suited her, with the exception of Ada and Signy, who had also come to say goodbye. Ingrid asked Eva Sofie:

"What are you howling at?"

"I don't know," Eva Sofie said, handing her a round tin with children's drawings on the lid of a Christmas tree and a number of rocking horses, it contained cakes and didn't fit into the suitcase, she had to carry it under her arm.

# 5

The initial part of the journey was by a combination of bus and truck, it was the first time Ingrid had been in a motorised vehicle, unless she had arrived at the hospital by the same means, this is the question she is asking herself now, with three other women, whom she can't remember, nor can she remember what clothes she was wearing.

The town had been bombed to pieces and burned down and was in such a dire state of recovery beneath half a metre of fresh snow that it looked like a rugged mountain landscape. They waded through what had once been a main street, Ingrid, two carers and Erik Falc, who had to collect a patient from the same boat that Ingrid would take, she knew he didn't usually do this himself.

He was carrying her suitcase, holding on to his hat and complaining about the weather, while Ingrid held her face up to the dry snow and felt it on her skin again. Around her head she had two scarves with the sou'wester she had been given by Eva Sofie on top, while the sturdy boots on her feet had enough room for three pairs of socks.

They were standing on the edge of the quay on the lookout for the boat in the misty harbour when Erik Falc suddenly said they should have their photographs taken.

Ingrid stared at him, both of their faces were bright red in the cold, so there was not a great deal she could read from the expression on his face, and the two carers were looking elsewhere.

"In these?" Ingrid said, indicating her clothes.

He nodded and said there was a photographer's on the corner, they were waiting for them, he wanted a souvenir.

"Of me?" Ingrid said.

He was unable to bring himself to say yes.

They left the carers, went through a door with condensation on the glass and into a pokey green room with a squat counter along one wall, on top of which was an empty vase, and a black wood-burning stove chugging away nicely in front of the other. A curtain behind the counter was pulled aside and a young man with black water-combed hair and red elastic sleeve garters came in and shook the doctor's hand, but not the lady's, her he sent only a discreet nod.

He ushered them towards a blossoming apple orchard in the sunset, made of cardboard and pinned to the back wall. They were asked to pose, each holding the back of a chair with a Gobelin seat and carved sides and legs. The distance between them should be equivalent to the width of the chair.

Ingrid took off her sou'wester, scarves and frieze jacket and knocked the ice out of her plaits while the photographer readied himself behind the tripod, and as she lifted her chin to concentrate, Erik Falc leaned over the back of the chair to whisper in her ear that, when all was said and done, she had been lucky, she had experienced love, he had not.

Ingrid could feel his breath and was looking at him as the flash went off, while Erik had turned back to the camera; the photograph had to be retaken.

They stared intently in the required direction as the snow melted on their clothes and ran to the floor of the apple orchard, the drips were audible before being drowned out by another flash, after which they could be heard again until a third flash well and truly dazzled them, whereupon the photographer straightened up, chewing his lower lip, and said:

"Let's take another one, shall we?"

Erik Falc Johannesen nodded. Ingrid Barrøy's mind was blank. They stared into the lens again waiting for the final flash and didn't look at each other when the photographer clapped his small white hands once and said bravo, nor when they were putting on their outdoor things and getting ready to go.

But after Erik had thanked the photographer and said a few words about payment and delivery and they were out in the liberating snow again, he became talkative and shouted in the wind that the skipper of the boat taking her south was a really tough character, for almost six months now he had transported refugees from Finnmark to various places down the coast and Ingrid would have to be prepared for rough conditions, the weather was already appalling. He also mumbled that he hoped she would drop him a line when she got home, without any spelling mistakes, he added, with what might have been a smile.

Ingrid nodded. He asked her again if she had anyone to go home to.

And Ingrid repeated:

"I do."

The boat didn't look like the sixty-foot whaler it was, but rather a floating warehouse, where people of all sizes wrapped up in so many layers of clothes they could scarcely move stood and sat and lay around, among suitcases and boxes and chests and furniture and sacks and mattresses. In the bows a wooden pole had been erected in the harpoon gun mountings and covered with a canvas tarpaulin, which stretched as far as the ship's rails on either side, and formed the ridge of a tent under which, judging by the number of boots, ten people lay. There was a huge commotion around a German soldier who punched a man repeatedly in the face until he fell backwards and lay on the deck howling.

The skipper flew out of the wheelhouse, looking as if he was going to pounce on the soldier, but controlled himself, the German didn't notice and just bent down and pulled the screaming man by his feet to a net that was used to load and unload goods, yelled something in German to the skipper, who turned his back on him in obvious contempt and then spotted Erik Falc and his party on the quay.

The skipper was a man in his early forties with thick, black hair, flecked with steel-grey, and an equally thick, chocolate-brown beard, bare-headed in sub-zero temperatures. He ignored the German and raised his arms in supplication to the doctor.

Erik Falc understood the gesture and gave a slight nod.

The skipper shrugged, went over to the winch and lowered the crane hook. The soldier grabbed the four corners of the net and attached them to it, and the writhing man was hoisted up onto the quay, where the carers extricated him from the net, got him to his feet and draped a jacket of the kind Ingrid was wearing over him. He hung limply in their arms, bleeding from his nose and a cut to the head. Erik Falc examined the injuries and asked him a few questions. The man shook his head. The carers led him to a waiting vehicle. The next moment the German soldier climbed up onto the quay, brushed the snow off his uniform and handed the doctor some rolled-up documents before unleashing a torrent of anger and striding off to the nearest storehouse, where troops were quartered.

"At least there won't be a guard on board then," Erik muttered, his head bowed and his eyes fixed on the papers. "That's something."

Ingrid wasn't listening.

She was on her knees inspecting the ladder the soldier had scaled, but it was low tide, four metres down to the deck, and there was ice on the rungs. A child shouted:

"She won't make it! She won't make it . . ."

Ingrid got to her feet and placed her suitcase and cake tin in the net that was still lying on the quay, stepped into the net beside them, lifted the lugs and, to Erik Falc's resigned, inaudible protests, looped them over the winch hook and called to the skipper to lower her onto the deck.

He shouted back, was she serious?

She shouted yes.

He smiled, grasped the levers and Erik watched the net close around his cured patient, who put her fingers through the top meshing, pulled the two sides together and was lifted like cargo, swung over the boat and slowly lowered to the deck to the cheers of the crowd of children who thronged around her and helped her out of the net – and Ingrid remembered she had left her sketch pad in the hideaway behind the closet wall in the South Chamber, under the eiderdown and rug, and that she was alone when she did so.

She also remembered something else: standing on a quay like this as a child and seeing her father arrive in her uncle's boat, him standing on the deck and smiling up at her, stretching out his arms and saying – nu tha's got t' hopp. She was three, four, five . . . it was three metres down, and she always jumped and he caught her, always.

Her fingers were numb with the cold. She brushed snow off her jacket and asked the skipper if he had any mittens. He had a think, went to the wheelhouse, lowered a window and threw out two coarse woollen mittens, heavy and felted, stiff with fish blood and guts, but warm and dry. She put them on and raised one of them, waved to Erik Falc, who was on the quay looking down at her with the expression she had woken up to so many times since she began to confide in him as with no other person, but no-one is perfect.

Erik Falc managed to raise his left glove to hip height and almost wave back, stared out across the agitated waters at the yawning gap between the moles at the opposite end of the harbour, placed his other gloved hand on his hat, turned and disappeared into the whirling snow that was falling like icing sugar on the boat and its passengers, while the skipper bellowed at the boys who had pulled in the mooring ropes, not to leave them in a pile on the deck, but coil them up tidily, he was bloody sick of telling them, you'd never believe they'd been to sea, the horse pizzles.

# 6

The *Salthammer* was a combined whaler and banker boat, and Ingrid was allocated a place on two layers of reindeer skin at the far end of the bait house next to a young mother, who cried as often as she drew breath, and four children, who didn't cry. The scuppers were jammed with rags, burlap and old clothes, there was rime frost on them as well as on the outermost bulkhead, whereas the bulkhead to the galley gave off a little heat. On the inside lay two-year-old Ante and four-year-old Mikkel, next came the two girls Ellen and Sara, who were five and eight, also lying head to foot, and the weeping mother, Anja, while Ingrid had to lie on the outside, the husband's place, he was the man who had been hoisted ashore when she came on board.

The family had been on the move for a week. Before that they had spent three months in a turf hut on the vast Finnmark plains, until, at around Christmas time, they could endure it no longer and walked down to a German garrison, convinced that they would be shot. Instead they were loaded onto a lorry and driven the three hundred kilometres to Hammerfest, which had been razed to the ground, whereafter they were put on board the *Salthammer*. None of them had had their clothes off for a month, until three days ago, when they were up in Risøyhamn, where they had all been allowed to have a bath in a military camp.

Ingrid asked whether there was a shower.

Anja nodded.

This was where her husband had his first breakdown, children always cope, she said in her rough dialect with its stress on every syllable, it is worse for us grown-ups. They were also given a delousing in Risøyhamn, and hot food. She said it was strange lice didn't freeze to death when humans did, and started to cry again, and consoled Mikkel, who had poked three fingers out of a hole in his mitten so he could chew them as he smiled at Ingrid.

Ingrid noticed a foul smell and asked if she was going to change him. Anja said it wasn't Mikkel, he was clean, but Ante, who messed himself twice a day, and she didn't have a change of nappy with her – didn't dare to ask for help either, the others on board would have nothing to do with her.

Ingrid said she would change the two-year-old.

Anja said it was too cold.

Ingrid said she would do it all the same.

The boy's crotch was burning red and he had caked shit all up his belly and back, but gazed at them with large, black eyes and said nothing. Ingrid asked if Anja had used the rags which were stuffed into the scuppers. Anja said yes. Ingrid said there was salt in them. Anja didn't understand.

"Salt," she repeated and told her to wrap up the toddler again and wait.

She got to her feet, went out along the deck, opened the door to the wheelhouse and shouted to the skipper, did they have any nappies on board? He turned and gave her a strange look.

"Yeah, yeah. Go and ask in the cabin."

Ingrid walked across the heaving deck, lifted the companion hatch and took three steps down into a steamy darkness stinking of vomit, where the mothers with small babies lay, as well as five orphans aged from three to eight. She asked if any of them had any nappies. No-one answered. She asked again and nobody answered. Ingrid said she needed some nappies. A young mother got up from the berth on the starboard side, stuck her face out into the light, and asked who the hell she was.

Ingrid stood there with a lump in her throat, on the verge of tears, until a nappy was thrust into her hands. She asked where they got their hot water. There was a chorus of laughter. A voice shouted: in the galley.

She walked back across the deck and into the galley, which was also full of children, lying in pairs, on the floor and on benches, as well as two adolescent boys who got up and looked as though they were intending to greet her. A large, old woman in black was sitting squeezed between a table screwed to the floor and the bulkhead, and was asleep, her toothless mouth agape. Girded by the metal fiddles on the roaring stove stood a voluminous coffee pot spewing white steam out of its swan-neck spout.

Ingrid asked whether there was water in it.

One of the boys said no, coffee. Ingrid said she needed some hot water. He looked at his mate, who leaned in the direction of a tap above a small sink, filled a kettle and jammed it tight against the coffee pot.

Ingrid waited. She asked them where they were from. Mehamn. Honningsvåg. Komagfjord. Tappeluft. Gamvik. Havøysund. Snefjord. Gjesvær. Rolvsøy. Skarsvåg . . . The old woman's blanket slipped to the floor, the youth who had put the kettle on the stove bent down and picked it up, shook it once and placed it over her again.

Ingrid asked who she was.

"It's Jadviga, our neighbour. She's Russian."

And the water had boiled.

Ingrid took care not to spill the water on her way back across the deck, which was rolling more and more, into the bait house, and told Anja to pull some more rags from the scuppers. Anja looked at her and said:

"They've got salt in them."

Ingrid laughed and told her to do so all the same.

She pulled out a brown felt sack, and seawater gushed in. Ingrid told her to stuff one of the reindeer skins in the scupper as she grabbed the sack, dipped it in the hot water and washed the boy, who was screaming in the freezing air, opened her blue suitcase and extracted Eva Sofie's bra. Anja almost stopped crying, and Sara asked what it was. Ingrid put it down and pulled out one of the pinafores, bit through the hem and ripped off two strips, folded them five times and laid them on top of each other around the boy's groin, then tied the nappy around them. Anja adjusted it, put on his old clothes and tucked him in under the sheepskin – and Ingrid recalled a fly which awoke on the window sill, buzzed feebly, then lay on its back and trod thin air with its six spindly legs and died; and how she picked it up between her fingertips, opened the window and threw it out, and this was just before they came back, Lensmann Henriksen and Leutnant Hargel, only the two of them, she could make out the boat in a grey bank of fog and hear their cries, two self-important men in a dory gliding slowly towards the island . . . But why had she been "bruised"?

Anja had laid a hand on her arm.

Ingrid asked if the children easily got seasick.

Anja said no, even though they had never even *seen* the sea before they boarded the *Salthammer*. Ingrid opened the cake tin and gave them a cake each, telling them they were called teacakes. They stared at them, gobbled them down and asked for more. She said they would have to wait, told Sara to keep an eye on the tin, got to her feet and went out again as a breaker swept over the aft quarter.

The weather had cleared up, the wind grew stronger the further from land they came, a biting north-easterly gale from dead aft, and still the men sat and stood on the deck, flapping their arms to keep warm, smoking and cursing. Ingrid went into the wheelhouse, where the skipper had his ear turned to the ceiling, listening, and pointed upwards as he spotted her, could she hear what it was, this sound, like tinkling glass?

She said yes.

"Hell and bloody damnation," he shouted. "Ice."

The sea ahead of them was open as far as the eye could see. The boat lurched forwards, was slowly sucked astern again, the metallic sounds from the roof intensified, the clatter of tools and other objects in the chart house, the engine's irregular knocking, he swore and asked whether Ingrid knew how to handle a boat.

She said yes.

"I knew it."

Without further ado he gave her the wheel, leaned forwards to the window pane and pointed at the green sector on a distant lighthouse due west, asked her three times if she could see the green sector, and wanted to hear a clear yes. Ingrid uttered something resembling a gasp, and he ran out.

No more than a few minutes later he was back, out of breath, he peered ahead towards the lighthouse and nodded, hawked back the phlegm in his throat, grabbed the helm and began to complain about having only country bumpkins on board, now they would have to knock off the ice as soon as the sea began to wash over the stern, look, he said nodding towards the glass behind them, it looked like thin, grey sheets of slate.

Ingrid asked him if he had any help on board.

Yes, he said, his nephew, Ole, he was a canny lad, but he was in the engine room taking care of the older kids, whom they kept there because of the heat. All of them had to go before the

Rations and Relocation Board in Ingrid's home parish, which would then allocate them to those farms which had room, it was a major operation, they were about to relocate a whole bloody province. His head sank between heavy shoulders and he said fortunately it had been a mild winter . . .

"Don't think we've introduced ourselves," he said, interrupting himself. "Magnus Mannvik. From Reine."

"Ingrid," Ingrid said, and mumbled something about her having some family in Reine, mentioned their names, too, but she had seen something in him she didn't like, the movements and fluster of a red-eyed, sleepless man out of kilter, she asked him if he ever got any sleep.

He laughed and muttered something about their having been up to Risøyhamn.

A huge swell dragged the deck in front of them down into a trough, they reached the bottom and were tossed up again to the sound of a distant howl. He cursed as they were thrown over the next breaker, gave her the helm, tore open the door and vanished once again.

Ingrid watched him walk, legs apart, down the wildly rolling deck, and zigzag from huddle to huddle, like a spider, as he shouted and gesticulated, yanking two figures to their feet and more or less dragging them aft and out of sight.

Ingrid tried to re-find the rhythm from her uncle's and father's fishing smacks, but this was a ship, and the conditions were impossible, the wheel jerked and snatched, the propeller left the water and the engine gave a hysterical roar. She was hurled against the bulkhead, wrenched the wheel in the wrong direction, the propeller got a hold again, and the boat reared as the door was torn open once more.

"Now they're knocking seven bells out of the ice."

He pushed her aside, placed a hand on the clutch lever and caught her eye, waited until she had found her balance and said calmly that she should put her right hand on his. Her head was whirring as she felt his cold knuckles beneath her fingertips while the bow plunged into another trough, he pulled the lever towards him, the engine eased, then the propeller left the sea again, he shoved the lever forwards once more as soon as the propeller bit, repeated the procedure through three more breakers, then stared enquiringly at her. She nodded mechanically and wanted to say yes, instead she said:

"I can't go home."

"*What?*"

He fixed her with his eyes.

"I can't go home."

She turned around, ran out and hung onto the bar outside the door, her feet dangling above the deck. A breaker washed over her, the keel was perpendicular to the crest of the waves, there was another scream from the engine, they were tilting from side to side. Ingrid let go of the bar and hit the deck, which was on the rise, she didn't attempt to get to her feet and clung to the bottom rung of the ladder and heard a voice somewhere in the spray above her:

"Go to the engine room and tell Ole to come up here."

She wanted to ask where the engine room was, but the wheelhouse door had already been slammed shut. She got up on her knees, was hurled against the rail and back towards the wheelhouse, grabbed a door handle, twisted it and her face was met by hot air from the pumps. She shouted into the darkness, and a face appeared, a young lad with a broad grin:

"How's it going?"

Ingrid yelled that he was to go to the wheelhouse, and concentrated on her next move. A long, quivering tremor shook the hull; the deck rose, listed and fell. She edged her way aft between six bodies lying on the deck banging off ice with wooden mallets, reached the back end of the stern, forced open the door of the bait house and saw Anja's terrified face, crawled in and lay with her arms around the girls, Anja hugged the boys to her.

"You're wet," Sara said.

Another tremor shook the hull, the arhythmic banging stopped, the *Salthammer* balanced on top of a new crest, the bait house veered towards port, before it slowly straightened up again, and a heavy slumber descended over the boat, a gasping for breath, which sounded like groans. Anja looked at her, panic-stricken.

"What is it now?"

Ingrid shook her head. The door opened and Magnus stuck his head in.

"We're on a stable keel now, we can probably make it to Arnøy, where there's a good harbour."

He glanced at the children, as if to count them, and was gone again. Anja sent Ingrid another searching look. Ingrid said everything would be fine, closed her eyes and buried her nose in Sara's hair, it smelled sweet and rancid, clasped her even more tightly and heard Anja repeat to Mikkel that everything would be fine. And then all that was left was the sounds, the engine and a distant, slow rocking – and Ingrid, who couldn't go home.

# 7

On Arnøy there was a school with two classrooms, an office for the teacher and a kitchen that was so small it was more like a recess. There was a chapel, five places where they processed fish, a ring of fishermen's shacks and boat sheds in addition to a number of small farms around a sheltered harbour, where the whole fleet was moored, with thick snow on the rails and wheelhouse roofs, and moustaches of green ice at the waterline.

Ingrid lay with Anja and the children in the school office, the first night on the floor, the next on the reindeer skins, now dry, both nights under blankets, they weren't cold and slept late into the morning.

It wasn't the first time the *Salthammer* had been here, the locals came with firewood and food, they were able to have a bath, and as the weather wasn't improving, they were also allowed to scrub their clothes in a wash-house next to the biggest fish-processing plant. Two elderly women turned up with a wheelbarrow full of old clothes, woollen slipper socks, nappies and twenty balls of grey yarn, and they wanted nothing for them. They were also given some talcum powder for Ante. And knitting needles. Ingrid taught Sara how to knit while Ellen watched. Anja's weeping had subsided into something more like regular sniffles and she said she hadn't been able to watch when her husband left the boat, had Ingrid seen what happened?

"Yes," Ingrid said. "He's alright now."

She counted the stitches and explained what she was doing, while Anja muttered on about the plague of lice and the insect spray and the rough treatment they had received in Risøyhamn, she was a Laestadian and considered having lice as shameful. Ingrid didn't know what a Laestadian was and said it was good they had got rid of the creatures.

Anja said:

"But we didn't have any lice. That was the whole point."

Ingrid talked to Sara about the knitting, praised her, put on her coat and told Mikkel to go with her to fetch some wood, she needed some air, some wind. They walked down the road to a boat shed where a load of cleft birch logs was stacked against the wall on the sheltered side and here they ran into Magnus, who was rested and half-drunk, and repeated what he had already said twice:

"You'd be better off sleeping with me and not the bloody Finns."

Ingrid hurried on.

He shouted something after them. She didn't hear what it was, this man who had been a busy black-marketeer before getting involved in the evacuation, a man who boasted of selling margarine for money and not ration coupons and transporting ten times more fish to the wholesalers in Trondheim than was officially declared, who seemed unmoved by the whole war or had made it his living – she stopped and looked around the freezing village: not a single person outdoors, but an island that was alive, with smoke from all the chimneys, the boats at their moorings, the day bitingly cold and the sky high above them like a dome of blue glass, the same sky that arched over Barrøy, and Ingrid didn't know where she was.

Mikkel stopped and looked up at her quizzically; both he and his sisters had bruises after the ordeal of crossing the fjord. Ingrid asked if it was hard. He nodded.

"You're strong."

She straightened the wood in his arms so it wouldn't fall and asked whether he missed his father.

At first he didn't seem to know what she meant. Then he said yes. Ingrid said they would soon have him back. Mikkel said yes again. Ingrid was pleased by everything he said. She asked if the blue bump on his forehead was painful. He said no. She said it would soon be gone, and they walked on in the bitter cold.

Ingrid was sitting on a reindeer skin with her back to the wall watching Ellen and Ante frolic like tentative, newly fledged eider ducklings on the sand-scrubbed floor. Anja boiled salted pork that Ingrid had bought from a blacksmith with some of the money Erik Falc had given her, old Malmberget's mysterious debt.

Anja had diced the meat. Then she had diced the potatoes and carrots and boiled them too long. Now she dipped crispbread into the pot and tasted it and looked around the crowd of children with the first hint of a smile that Ingrid had seen on her hollowed face, this was a woman of that indefinable war-ravaged age, somewhere between twenty-five and sixty, as though not only her husband and life had abandoned her, but also the seasons, and still she had *something* that Ingrid didn't have, a simple, uncompromising clarity, an unmistakeable misfortune, visible and tangible, not just a swirl of elusive, confused images and emotions she couldn't reconcile.

Ingrid heard Erik Falc's words, about her having found love when it was there and grasping it, but the truth was that she hadn't grasped anything at all, she had just been who she was when it happened, someone she wasn't anymore – and she hadn't bled for two months now.

*That* was what she should have asked Eva Sofie, could she trust the days she had spent at the hospital, the way they were marshalled and presented on the board by the window, she should have gone through them hour by hour, reviewed and scrutinised not only the days on Barrøy that were unaccounted for, but also her body – *after* she had arrived at the hospital.

She got up and pressed her fingertips on the desk, beneath all manner of pull-down charts on frayed canvasses, the strings dangling around her head, Anja looked at her with questions in her eyes.

Ingrid looked back.

"I can't go home."

Anja stood up and took her by the arm. Ingrid repeated the words, tore herself away, went into the kitchen, stood there trembling, grabbed six large tablespoons from the drawer, went back, sat with the children, stuck one spoon in the pot and stirred aimlessly, lifted her catch and blew on it until it was cool enough to put to Ante's lips, Ante whom she had taken onto her lap without noticing. He opened his mouth, smacked his lips and wanted more, he was the only one with no bruises, his skin was unblemished, and he smiled. Ingrid lowered the spoon again and saw that her hands weren't trembling, she had a feeling that Anja, too, noticed she wasn't trembling and that she breathed a sigh of relief, and they smiled at one another.

# 8

The morning they were to continue their voyage south was clear and windless. An invisible sun spread copper and brass over the snow atop the mountains on the mainland. On board, there was a festive mood without festivities, a muted, dejected and hopeful sense of order, the beginning of a new life, the most fragile of all.

The blacksmith who had sold Ingrid the pork at a steep price came aboard and helped them to seal the scuppers in the bait house, laid the dry reindeer skins over the floor and also gave them three rugs that weren't new, but were thicker than those they already had. Anja shook his hand and thanked him, and Ingrid said he'd already had his payment.

Magnus came in, muttering that his bait house looked like a boudoir, and said that if the weather held there might be enough room for the older kids here too, the ones who had been in the engine room, did the blacksmith have any more rugs?

The man looked down, didn't answer, and left.

Magnus shook his head and asked whether Ingrid wanted some coffee:

"We *have* coffee!"

Ingrid said they would both like some and began to make a barrier against the outer bulkhead using the blue suitcase, the sack of grey woollen yarn and the cake tin she had filled with crispbread, also purchased from the blacksmith, who returned soon after with half a seine net on his back, old, but dry and smelling of tar.

She asked what he was going to do with it.

"It's good quality," he said, as he cleared away everything they had set up, spread out the net over the floor, three layers of it, put back the skins and rugs and returned Ingrid's suitcase and cake tin to the position they had been in before.

Ingrid said thank you, but it was rugs they needed, and skins.

Magnus arrived carrying two dirty coffee mugs, gave one to Anja and the other to Ingrid, cast his eye around the bait house and looked as though he was planning to repeat what he had said about it being like a boudoir, then shook his head, raced along the deck and shouted something down to the engine room.

His nephew, Ole, and three youths came up and stood alongside the ship's rail as if before a priest. The blacksmith laughed at the sight of so much soot and oil, wished them a safe journey and went ashore again.

Ingrid noticed that the oldest, a lad of maybe sixteen, was staring out to sea with his left eye, which was red. She realised he was blind in this eye and asked how it had happened. He lowered his right eye and said they were from Hammerfest, Skarsvåg to be precise, as if that were explanation enough; the other two, Sverre and Helmer, were his brothers. Ingrid repeated the question, and he said something about a red ember when the town went up in flames, his parents were dead.

She asked what his name was.

"Arne."

Arne was tall and lanky, with broad, bony shoulders, which projected forwards like a yoke; his tar-brown hair was greasy and as long as a girl's, and some green matter was running from his left nostril. Ingrid presumed his state had something to do with the same fire and asked him whether he had been to see a doctor. He said no and looked down at the deck with his living eye and at her with the dead one. She made a spontaneous movement, as if to get him to rediscover her presence, nodded at a kitbag and an oil-stained cloth bundle on the deck between them and asked whether that was all they had?

"Yes."

She said they could sleep between the others and the bait-house door, and exchanged glances with Anja, who put her coffee mug down on the ship's rail and rushed inside and began to arrange the children on the reindeer skins as if to lay claim to them.

Ingrid glanced over at Ole, who was still standing there, and asked him if the crew had any blankets. He shrugged. Ingrid told the brothers to wait, walked over to Magnus, who was on the foredeck surrounded by a crowd of men, and asked him if *he* had any blankets. No, he said curtly, but shook his shoulders and adopted that blank expression which meant that he was not only searching for a solution, but would also find one.

"Try that bloody blacksmith again. We'll wait."

Ingrid scrambled ashore and ran in the direction of the village, caught up with the blacksmith and asked him if he could sell them some more blankets, rugs, sheepskins . . .

"Sell?" he said slowly, fixing his eyes on her.

"Yes, sell. We're desperate."

"You must be loaded."

"No," Ingrid said.

"How much will you pay?"

She told him she'd give the same amount as last time, per blanket per skin. He chewed on it. She increased the offer by half a krone, per skin. He smiled, turned and hurried up to the village. Ingrid trudged back, clambered aboard and went over to the brothers at the stern. All she could get out of them was that the two older boys had worked as carpenters with their father. She asked them how old they were. Sverre was twelve and Helmer ten. Ingrid had no more questions. Oh yes, she did, hadn't it been hot down in the engine room?

"Yes."

"And wasn't it noisy?"

They looked at one another, as if considering whether this was worth answering and concluding it wasn't. Ingrid poured the coffee grounds into the sea, watched them sink and disperse like ants across the green, sandy bottom, looked down into the mugs, but couldn't think of anything else to say and led the boys into the galley, where the same youths as before were taking care of old Jadviga from Russia, who looked as though she couldn't decide whether to fall asleep or stay awake. Ingrid asked if they had any more water.

"Yes, fresh water," as much as she wanted.

She rinsed the mugs under the tap, looked around for a cloth that wasn't there, put the mugs in the sink and asked them where they came from.

"Mehamn."

"Was that burned down, too?"

"Yes."

Ingrid wondered whether they were brothers, and where their parents were, what kind of work they had done, as if she had been set down on this earth to carry out a survey of people who had been driven out of their homeland, since nothing made sense inside herself, but before any answers were forthcoming – they didn't look like brothers, more like friends, closer than any relatives – she saw through the porthole that the blacksmith was back on the quay. She ran to the prow.

"Just sling 'em on board," Magnus said. He was standing in the midst of the same crowd of men, all staring at the new arrival, half-smoked fags in their mouths and puffs of smoke dispersing in the clear, cold air.

"And the money?" the blacksmith shouted.

"It's coming."

The blacksmith hesitated, dumped three moth-eaten sheepskins onto the deck, raising a cloud of dust, then two new-looking rugs and three grey woollen blankets, which fluttered down like sails. Magnus waited until the last had landed, signalled to the boy who was always with Ole and was now at the bow.

He jerked the mooring rope upwards with a flourish, causing the loop to slip off the bollard on the quay. Another boy was standing on the bait-house roof at the stern and performed the same piece of magic with the aft mooring rope. Magnus himself unhitched the spring line and glanced up at Ole in the wheelhouse. Ingrid realised she had missed something. Ole engaged the clutch and gave full throttle, the *Salthammer* heeled over, almost sending her flying, and ploughed across the mirror like surface of the harbour, dividing the village into two with a foaming furrow of a wake.

Magnus waved to the blacksmith, who stood motionless. The men laughed. Ingrid bent down to pick up the skins and blankets.

"Shall I help you, young lady?" Magnus shouted in her ear.

The crowd of men laughed even louder, the puffs of smoke, their shamefaced, evasive eyes. Magnus held a hand in the air, directed a black finger at the man laughing loudest and told him to pick up the skins and help her.

"Pronto."

# 9

It was night when they docked at the trading post. Anja and the children were asleep, also the two younger Skarsvåg brothers, Sverre and Helmer. But Ingrid and Arne were woken by the engine stopping and went on deck in the steely-blue darkness, it was windless and snowing lightly. Magnus and one of the men stood by the rail smoking, a little further away sat Ole and his friend on the foredeck talking in low voices in the silence.

Magnus gave her the mug he was holding. She turned it and took a mouthful of lukewarm coffee. He smiled.

"Your home-ground?"

Ingrid nodded from behind a glass wall, the landing stage beneath the quay, the Little Quay, where she moored when she was going to buy her provisions or work at the trading post, the steps up through the hole in the quay and the snow that settled on her hair and shoulders and bare hands, on her clothes and the rim of the coffee mug, turning into drops of water she slurped into her mouth until she checked herself, because

Magnus was watching her with eyes that were impossible to avoid.

"So you don't want to go home?"

She recoiled, gave back the mug and brushed the snow from her hair and shoulders, she was wearing neither a headscarf nor a sou'wester, but following Eva Sofie's patented method she had knotted her two plaits behind her head to hide the scars, water dripped from her eyelashes, she felt cold and feverish. She looked down at some rolled-up papers he was holding and asked what they were. He told her to guess. She said:

"Do you never sleep?"

He gave her the papers, like crew lists, with the names of the evacuees and information about the homes where they were to be placed, the farms, houses and boat sheds in the village that the Rations and Relocation Board had gained access to and where they had been assured there was room.

Two lines caught her eye, because she was searching for the first and was surprised by the second: Anja and the children were going to the rectory, which was empty, together with two of the mothers at the front of the cabin, with infants, and two men whose names didn't mean anything to her. The surprise was the signature, that of Lensmann Henriksen, not in his capacity as a lensmann, but as the Chairman of the Board, and Ingrid realised it could hardly be a promotion. Magnus stared at her with interest.

She said straight out that this man had collaborated with the Germans.

"Perhaps he's smart."

"What?"

"He saw the end was coming for the Jerries."

She gave that some thought.

"And what do *you* think?"

He threw back his head and laughed.

"I'm a communist. The Russkies are going to win!"

Ingrid was about to laugh along with him, but decided her mouth was too open, so she closed it and looked down for the few seconds it took, then turned to Arne, but could sense that the apathy in his dead eye was affecting his healthy one, so she had no choice but to turn back to Magnus, and she asked him where the brothers were going.

He asked what their names were.

Arne mumbled Isaksen, from Skarsvåg, but they had lived for a while in Hammerfest. Magnus pointed to the papers and Ingrid saw that the three Skarsvåg Isaksens were going to a farm in the south of the main island, Molandsvika. She said:

"They're nice."

Arne looked as if he had been enough trouble and wanted to go. Ingrid held him back, and mumbled, her eyes averted:

"At least I *think* they're nice, they're old."

His right eye looked past her, sceptical. She felt a touch of remorse and had to look at Magnus again, a man at his peak even at three in the morning, she drew a deep breath, gave him back the papers and said she knew where Henriksen lived, she could show him the way if he liked?

He declined, they should wait and let the people have a

good night's sleep, went into the galley and re-emerged with two mugs of coffee, gave her one and Arne the other. The boy bowed in gratitude, took a swig, it was too hot, placed two large fists around the mug and went quickly back to the bait house.

Ingrid wanted to follow him, but instead subjected herself to even more silence in the company of a man. They waited. Ingrid said she had to go back to the children. He shrugged. She asked if he had heard about a ship sinking a bit further south, a troop ship?

He said no.

Ingrid thought that strange. After all he had a radio, didn't he?

He looked at her in surprise.

"So, I've got a radio, have I?"

"Yes," Ingrid said, she had seen it in the chart room.

He smiled it off and asked her why she was interested in a ship going down, it was probably a military secret, wasn't it?

She said she thought there was something else.

Magnus asked what that might be, but at the same instant turned to Ole, who was still lying on the foredeck chatting with his friend, and shouted something Ingrid didn't catch. She didn't catch Ole's answer either, the three men laughed, which again gave her the feeling that she had missed something, that she still wasn't herself.

# 10

The first fishing boats came in and backed away from the trading post as Magnus refused to move the *Salthammer*. When at length Henriksen made an appearance, and became aware of the commotion, he apologised for being late and was awkward and servile. Magnus enquired whether the Chairman had slept well and asked for proof of identity, then once again declined to move his boat so the fishermen could get to the cranes.

"We need to use the Little Quay."

Henriksen and his men went down the steps and on board and produced lists of names which matched those that Magnus had on his. The Chairman's eyes softened when he spotted Ingrid.

"Ah, it's you."

Ingrid said nothing. Henriksen shook his head and continued to confer with Magnus, who had got Ole to summon the refugees on deck, with all their belongings, in the falling snow it resembled a silent Mass. Henriksen read out the names in turn, names he was hardly able to pronounce, issued instructions and warnings, occasionally a key, and demanded signatures, which he attempted to say something humorous about as they were scribbled down, a venture he eventually discontinued when he began to realise that the amusement was not shared.

A few sniffles could be heard from women saying goodbye to one another. Together with their children and mattresses and chests and suitcases, they were helped up onto the quay, where two motor cars and five horses and carts had assembled to transport them to their new homes.

The men didn't sniffle, one by one they shook Magnus by the hand in that heartfelt yet shamefaced silence that a man struggles to maintain when he knows he has something fundamental to be thankful for, such as his life.

Ingrid also wanted to say thank you, to Anja and the children, for without them she wouldn't have made it here, which of course wasn't anything to be thankful for, and was gripped by a new bout of panic, she snatched at Henriksen's keys, called to Anja and nodded to the two men standing at his side.

Henriksen asked why she was interfering and went on to study first the family, then the two sets of papers, for there were a few things wrong here, Finns and Lapps should be kept separate from Norwegians.

Anja yelled that she was a person of fixed abode, not a nomad, she was a farmer's wife. Henriksen laughed once again, and looked around for support. Magnus didn't laugh, he said:

"Well, they're well and truly mixed now, after this trip."

Ingrid, Anja and the children walked up towards the village accompanied by the men, the mothers with the babies and two young orphaned girls, who were dragging a shared cloth sack, past the store, where Margot and two others stood outside in the winter cold watching them. Margot caught sight of Ingrid and waved. Ingrid waved back. She didn't see any soldiers, nor any military vehicles, the camp was as deserted as the rectory.

"Now you're going to get a decent house to live in," she said feverishly, as she unlocked the rectory door and told the two men to fetch wood and coke and get the fire going in all the stoves, walked from room to room with her snow-covered entourage at her heels and presented all the things she still recognised, down to the smallest detail, without it causing her pain.

She also got to see the babies for the first time; throughout the journey the women had just looked pregnant, but as the temperature rose the babies were now unwrapped from their shapeless garments and had bright eyes and pink, hairless heads in their new home.

The two mothers installed themselves in their separate rooms on the first floor, where confirmands from the nearby islands used to sleep in twos. Ingrid also knew where there was a cradle in the attic. She escorted Anja to the priest's bedroom, he didn't usually sleep with his young wife, but still had the widest bed. She assigned the two orphaned girls to the wife's bedroom, the bed there was wide, too; she showed them the eiderdowns and cupboards and drawers, and asked them if they had anything else with them apart from the sack, which they were still carrying between them.

They said no.

She asked if they were sisters.

One said no, the other hesitated.

Mikkel was given the room Ingrid had used when she was waiting to be confirmed. One of the men commandeered the priest's study, which was called the library, and where there was an English leather sofa. The other man moved into the wing where they usually housed guests. There were still two vacant bedrooms. Ingrid thought for a moment, fetched Sara and Ellen and said they could have one each. They exchanged glances. Sara said:

"We want to be together."

Ingrid nodded and summoned everyone to one room, told them to sit on the beds and explained that when they went to the store with coupons and money, which they had just been given by the Board – and she would soon be giving them more – then Margot would say what use were money and coupons when she had no margarine. But Margot did have margarine, so they shouldn't believe her, she preferred to sell it without coupons, at a higher price, unless of course she had sold out, but in that case she had also sold it for money, or at a higher price than the margarine normally should cost.

Anja couldn't make head nor tail of this.

One of the young mothers could.

Ingrid emphasised that when they went to the store, for

sugar or flour or lamp oil, they should never pay the price asked, but haggle, both with and without coupons, and shrink from nothing, especially when money was involved. And when they bought fish at the trading post they should pay a little more than the foreman asked for, unbidden, and not use coupons, as they would then get more fish next time, or else buy direct from the boats, and remember that herring is cheap, it is almost free, though at the moment it was scarce . . .

Ingrid was resolute and febrile, she looked at Sara with a worried expression and said she would have to start school at once. Sara nodded. Ingrid looked at Anja and said the same. Didn't she trust her, Anja said.

Ingrid ignored the tone in her voice and asked the two girls how old they were. One of them said six, the other didn't answer, but she looked older.

"You have to go to school, too."

The girl didn't react. Ingrid was about to ask what her name was, but one of the young mothers broke in and said she knew them and would see to it that the older girl – whose name was Nelvy, it emerged – started school; the other girl was called Gunvor, they were both from a village near Bjørnevatn, but hadn't been down the mineshaft.

Ingrid asked what that was supposed to mean.

The mother said the inhabitants of Kirkenes had taken shelter in a mine when the town was reduced to rubble, but many of them, including the families of Nelvy and Gunvor, had been shipped west, not all of them had made it, she didn't know why, they never said anything, neither Nelvy nor Gunvor . . .

"And now you can try to take off her hat," she shouted to Ingrid. "Cos I can't!"

Puzzled, Ingrid looked from the woman to the hat Nelvy was clasping to her head with both hands.

"What's all this about?"

At this point one of the men had had enough, he was in his late sixties, had hollow cheeks with white stubble, a mouth that was far too big for the few teeth he had, and he was shaking violently; he began by clearing his throat, then stretched out an arm and said: enough of this jabber, before tearing off the girl's hat and tossing it into a corner. She screamed: she had mange and not a hair on her bony head. Ingrid watched as the girl ran around the bed and grabbed the hat, waited until she had put it on again and told Nelvy to follow her.

"Is there any work for us here?" the old man yelled after her. "We need work."

Ingrid looked at him.

"Otherwise we'll go crazy."

The mother who had told Ingrid about the mineshaft turned her back on them and began to breastfeed her baby. The children ran outside, one by one. Anja undressed Ante. Ingrid stood with her hand locked around Nelvy's wrist and asked the man if he was ill, as he was shaking. He shrugged. She said she would enquire at the trading post, there was always work to do there, or at the canning factory.

He said he was a carpenter.

Then he knew what hard work was, Ingrid said, and went down to the wash-house with Nelvy in tow. There was running water here, and two large stone wash basins were bolted to the wall, there was a stove, too. Ingrid filled one of the bowls, put it on the stove and told her that here she, Ingrid, was the boss; Nelvy could choose between being washed with or without her hat on. Nelvy wept and opted to keep it on, after some pressure to do the opposite.

When the water was hot, Ingrid bent the girl over the bowl, poured two ladles of water over the hat, put down the ladle, pulled off the hat and held Nelvy in a vice-like grip while she scooped more water over her and scrubbed her head with carbolic soap.

Nelvy squirmed and screamed, but gradually became more submissive as Ingrid poured water over her. She scrubbed her again and rinsed her for a third time. She didn't see any lice, and now it didn't look as if she had any mange either, only those strange bumps on her scalp.

Ingrid wrapped a tea towel around the girl's head, put the hat in the basin and washed it too with carbolic soap, on the washboard, while Nelvy perched on the edge of the other basin watching her, both hands holding the tea towel, it looked like a turban, her fingers were long and slender.

Ingrid said they would dry the hat over the kitchen stove, it wouldn't take long, in the meantime she could wear another. She took her up to one of the children's rooms, where there was a chest of drawers full of clothes, and fished out a blue hat.

Nelvy's was red. She wanted a red one. Ingrid rummaged round in the drawer and found a grey one. Nelvy nodded reluctantly and wanted to put it on over the towel. Ingrid said it looked nice. Gunvor was standing in the doorway and said it looked peculiar. Nelvy didn't seem to mind. Ingrid grabbed her slender fingers and sat gazing at them in puzzled admiration until Nelvy retracted them with a shy smile, then asked Ingrid what her name was.

Ingrid told her, and added that she lived on Barrøy, then asked her in turn what her name was, apart from Nelvy. Nelvy said she thought she was called Arvola.

Ingrid asked why she hadn't said so before, now there was nothing about her in the Rations and Relocation Board's papers. Nelvy said she didn't know. She asked where Barrøy was.

"There," Ingrid said, pointing at the wall above one bed, where there hung a picture of a smocked shepherd with a crook and three goats, which Nelvy sat staring at.

Ingrid told her she had to go and inspect the larder, left Nelvy and went downstairs and in between the rows of preserves, pickles and canned food. She sat down on the lowest shelf, where the priest's wife kept her copper kettles and tubs of oats and flour, and was forced to acknowledge that she couldn't put it off any longer. Moreover she was worn out, on the verge of tears, she stared blindly at bread boxes and colanders of all shapes and sizes, and thought about Nelvy's fingers, and about the blue suitcase, the cake tin and the sack of woollen yarn, which were still aboard the *Salthammer*, the way forwards.

She shuddered, went out again, locked the door and gave the key to the young mother who knew her way around the black market, asked what her name was.

"Johanna . . ."

Nineteen-year-old Johanna Matea Hætta from the pine barrens in Tverredalen was thereby appointed master of the keys and the larder in an affluent rectory with a view of the sea; she pulled a thread from her skirt, tied the key around her neck and carried on breastfeeding without a word before the eyes of Ingrid, who felt obliged to direct her gaze past both her and the baby.

She gave Ellen and Sara a quick hug, told them to go and play with Nelvy and Gunvor, reminded Nelvy once again that she had to start school, heard Anja ask what was wrong with her, and rushed out into the snow with an irksome sense that she was past the point of no return, she felt it in her knee joints, in the form of a kind of quivering.

She was given as much margarine and sugar as she wanted by Margot, who remarked that Ingrid war looken' in fein fettle. In exchange for coupons and money. But she didn't respond to Margot's questions about how she had been doing, just hurried out and wheeled the goods down the road at an ever increasing speed, slowed down when the masthead lantern and crow's nest of the *Salthammer* came into view above the trading post's roof, put one foot before the other across the snow and ice, rigid and cautious, the hefty weight of the cart yoke against her back.

They had moved the boat back against the quayside; in front of the trading post a local fisherman was unloading his catch while two other boats were waiting, the eyes that were trained on her from the quay, recognising her, some waves, some shouts, she waved back and walked at a measured pace down the twelve steps to the Little Quay and yelled across the empty deck of the *Salthammer* that she had come to say goodbye.

No reaction.

She shouted again, heard faint laughter from somewhere above her and spotted Magnus at the wheelhouse window, his brown beard, his hair, his eyes that were looking out and up into the air. The deck was swabbed and shiny, the canvas tent had been removed from the harpoon cannon mountings, the wooden pole was gone, and the ship's engine was running.

Ingrid wished them a good trip north.

He answered something she didn't catch. She shouted:

"What?!"

He yelled through the noise of the engine:

"Your things."

The suitcase and the cake tin in the bait house. She looked down at her box of provisions, lifted it quickly over into the boat, stepped aboard and ran to the stern as Ole loosened the hawsers at the prow and Magnus revved the engine so the bow was propelled outwards. Without displaying any emotion she watched Ole go back and unhitch the other rope, everything repeats itself, but it was her own decision, that didn't make it any easier, there was no turning back now, though there was no relief to be found.

*

Ingrid swung herself up the two rungs to the wheelhouse and said she would guide him out.

"Foul waters ahead?"

"No."

She qualified her answer: "A bit."

He said:

"Thought you didn't want to go home?"

"No."

Then, staring rigidly ahead at the familiar fairway, she said he should go with her up onto the island and spend the night with her there, but have a wash first. He was silent for a long time and then asked:

"Where?"

"In the tub!"

He chuckled, and they said no more.

He took them north-west of Oterholmen and ploughed through an armada of eider ducks between the northern headland and the harbour, mumbled some complimentary words about the new quay, this mountain of hand-hewn pink stone built by foreign hand some time in Ingrid's childhood, when there was also a war. She said, yes, it was a fine quay.

They left the boat in the hands of Ole and his mate, who had sabotaged his existence as a refugee and enlisted on the *Salthammer* for good. Something was said between the men, which Ingrid didn't catch. She walked with Magnus up towards the unlit house, she at the front with the suitcase and the cake tin, her eyes bored into the thick snow, as if once more looking for tracks that weren't there, he carrying the provisions and balls of yarn, into the cold, lifeless kitchen, here too she managed to keep herself blind.

She lit the lamps, and he got the fire going while she blinked her eyelids and found nothing to fear. When he had nothing more to put his hands to, she stood still in front of him until they were both embarrassed, and began to undress him, even though it was not yet warm in the kitchen, she ignored some strained witticisms about the zinc tub that had served the Barrøyers for generations, and washed him without a word, while she thought about Nelvy and water, running, purifying, soothing water, cold, hot, smooth, wet, salty . . . while she thought of soap that didn't lather, of odours and muck, until finally she was able to give an exploratory sniff and detect not the slightest trace of a human body.

He said:

"Why are you doing this?"

She stripped down to her waist, showed him her back and asked what he thought of the scars. He said they seemed to be healing well. She changed the water, told him about Nelvy and those long, slender fingers of hers and then began to *talk* about water too, as though driven by some elevated form of purification, a ritual that had to be repeated in order to have any effect, while he sat swathed in a blanket in the rocking chair and asked his question once again:

"Why are you doing this?"

"I have to."

She pulled him upstairs to the South Chamber and lay with him without a word, apart from repeating the answer to his question, and she thought that his asking no fewer than three times made him a better person.

After he had fallen asleep, she got up, went down to the kitchen and washed, yet again, now without a thought in her head, climbed the stairs to the North Chamber, lay in the cold bed, fell asleep and didn't wake until the night had passed and a new winter's day was pressing hard against the white window-panes. By then the *Salthammer* had left Barrøy. Ingrid wondered where Koshka the cat was, and realised that the eagle must have taken her, at least that was a bearable thought. Then she fell asleep again.

# III

# 1

In the late summer when Ingrid Barrøy turned ten, her father took the whole family with him to Nesholmen to buy hay. Nesholmen was so close to the mainland that it didn't seem like an island. They sounded as if they were going on holiday, her mother called it a picnic and had to explain to them what that meant, it was a red-letter day in a calendar with only black ones.

"But hvor will thar bi room f'r th' hay?"

"We'll teik two boats."

It had been the wettest summer in living memory. But at the end of August such a ferocious heatwave descended over land and sea that minds were sapped and everyone's eyes swam. A sweltering haze hung over the loam-black fields, the birds were silent, the countryside heaved inaudible groans and the sea shone like a newly varnished floor.

Ingrid's mother babbled excitedly and packed her father's Lofoten chest with food and milk and rainwear they hoped wouldn't be needed. They climbed into the færing and towed the rowing boat and took turns at the oars, stood up and rocked the craft from side to side, laughed and fooled around, in the hours it took to reach Nesholmen, where Hans Barrøy haggled for some of last year's hay with an elderly couple who no longer kept livestock but still mowed their meadows.

The old man asks if they want some coffee.

They drink it on the grass. They eat and chat while Ingrid and Lars play with the dog in the farmyard. They load the hay onto the rowing boat and lash it down.

But they don't call the children when they have finished, instead they lie down in the sand, supported on their elbows, and look out to sea – to Barrøy, they idle their time away.

Hans Barrøy remembers he has brought a bottle along, from which first the men, then the women drink. They strip off for a dip, and it is easier for a child to be naked, so it's difficult to persuade their grandfather Martin, the only person who can't swim; he takes off his clothes and sits on the shore like a white fish, gets up and walks slowly down to the lapping tongues of water, wades a few steps in and curses the insects on his back he can't reach with his large copper-brown hands, until the others have had enough, then he emerges from the water and gets dressed with them, and they continue to sit around on the beach.

The couple at the farm have seen what they are doing and come down to join them, they have a bottle, too.

This is a scene drawn by a child, the green is green, the blue is blue, hardly a sea urchin is red here, but it is the yellow that makes the most lasting impression, and the white sand. Nesholmen is perhaps a little bigger than Barrøy, and there may be two or three households on it, but if the truth be told the two islands are as like as like can be; the Barrøyers are among their own kind, it is a marvel of a day, until this one, too, draws to an end, and they have to go home.

Hans rows, with the placid oar strokes of a contented man. He is wearing a black waistcoat with a watch chain without a watch, and a captain's cap, which his brother doesn't allow him to wear in Lofoten. Then Barbro and Maria row for a while. They are wearing their finest clothes, one in yellow, the other in blue, as always, they have woollen jumpers hanging around their shoulders, and their oars are silent spoons in a thick sauce. The boats' long shadows glide over those of the mountains, and the tow rope bobs quietly between them, it is so quiet that the voices carry from the færing to the rowing boat behind, to the children and old Martin, who has fallen asleep on the hay: it is Hans Barrøy telling Maria they should also have had a son, didn't she think, a playful invitation from a tipsy man to a beautiful woman. Maria says they have Lars, and Ingrid sees Barbro smiling down on the boards. She also notices that Lars isn't listening, he is asleep in the crook of his grandfather's arm, and she thinks she will have to do him in.

She straightens up sharply, the voices in the færing are muted, her mother turns to face her and asks if she is cold. Ingrid says no. They smile at each other in light that is becoming even bluer.

# 2

Now the light from the torches in the sea rises, like sleep-inducing swirls, indistinct, flickering images, and with it the first terror Ingrid felt, emanating from within herself, a personal poison which hitherto she has managed to suppress – until she finds herself lying on her back in her parents' bed in the South Chamber, both hands covering her face, filled with the same raging fear; at her side the closet door is wide open, the eiderdown and rug have been flung aside, and the sketch pad has gone.

She sits up, stares at the gaping door and lies down again.

She has chopped firewood with a blunt axe, because she cannot both whet the axe and turn the grindstone alone, she has baked bread and now needs milk, she has scrubbed the floors of rooms where nobody stays, she has seen that the potatoes in the cellar have survived the winter frost. She has cleared a path through the snowdrifts between the buildings, even though she has no animals to tend. She has wandered around the island like the hands on a clock face, without discovering any signs of change, nor what she needs in order to be whole again.

She closes the closet door and stands motionless, pondering. Then she walks into the next room, lifts objects and weighs them in her hand, a chamber pot, a dish, a picture of a lamb, she fingers an embroidered tablecloth, pulls out a drawer and pushes it in again, so gently that it hardly seems to move. She stares out through the window until everything turns to water, then goes down to the larder and removes three jars of preserves which have cracked in the frost, separates the glass from the berries and throws the fruit away, carries out the broken glass and knows where to bury it until the spring, she goes into the cowshed and sits on the steps where she once saw some drops of water without understanding what this meant.

A boat with two men, and their laughter.

The boat was a dory and the men were Lensmann Henriksen and Leutnant Hargel: Henriksen struggled shakily to his feet and threw out the mooring rope, but not far enough, Hargel's raucous jeers; Ingrid waded out and pulled them onto the skids, Henriksen fell forwards with a thump; she saw him fall and heard him curse, a body hitting the forepeak of the boat, more hollow laughter, distant, and then in the house . . .

They had returned to check up on something, they had come to interrogate her, because of a suspicion, they had come to beat the truth out of her, if necessary, and to do something else, which she can't remember.

She gets up from the cowshed steps, goes inside the house for some more clothes, puts out the boat and rows on the seaward side of Moltholmen and does something while nothing is happening inside herself and she has to start to pin her hopes on the admonishing letter she wrote to Suzanne having its desired effect, the letter she ought to have sent to Lars, for she cannot be alone, less so now than ever before – the fishing line glides over the bow roller and disappears into the sea, re-emerges at the next tug, and a shower of spray falls over mittens and thwart and rail, but it doesn't turn to ice.

She stares intently at the drops of water. And realises she hasn't got warm from the work, but because the wind has turned, and it did so a long time ago, as the snow was already wet when she walked down to the boat shed, and in the south there is a column-shaped cloud rising to the sky.

She rows back at top speed and puts the boat out of harm's way, boards up the shed, carries her catch to the house, guts and cleans the fish in the kitchen, sees to the liver and roe, cooks some food and eats until the crashing of the storm becomes unbearable.

She lies on the kitchen floor with an eiderdown over her head, feels the house shaking, and is struck on the temple by a rubber cosh resembling a black snake, which is lifted again and hits her above the ear and on the cheek, several white flashes and a lasting silence that fades into a distant sound of running water, and it isn't clean, it is urine, and it is hers, the hot smell of herself, her nostrils filling with blood . . .

They had found the sketch pad.

*

The rain was lashing against the roof and walls. She got up and vomited, lay down again and slept in the kitchen until the island had become a gleaming armour-plate of brown ice. She rose to her feet and went out into the last gusts of wind, watched the weather clearing above the mountains in the east, the sun an inflamed eye above the horizon in the south, she was at the end of the road, if Suzanne was ever going to come, it had to be now. But the days passed, and the nights, and vanished without trace, and it was Barbro who came.

# 3

Barbro was rowed over by Adolf from Malvika and his son Daniel. With them they also had a sack of flour, a churn of milk and a ewe in lamb. Ingrid had watched them coming for more than an hour without a thought in her head, without any expectations.

Now she watched her aunt step over the gunwale and hobble ashore and kneel down and with excited whoops kiss the ground. Ingrid could hear Daniel laughing and watched as Adolf eased the sheep over the side of the boat and into the sea. She waded out and dragged it ashore, where it stood shaking itself like a dog. She laughed without doing so, straightened up and looked straight at them, and they looked back as if they recognised her, and she said it was good to see them, what date was it?

They said it was the second week in February.

"Wednesday."

Ingrid was told that Barbro had paid for the sheep with money, and for the milk and flour, but they would like the churn back.

They carried it up between them and emptied the contents

into one of Barrøy's pails while Barbro sang and waved her arms about and cried and said hallelujah and made such a fool of herself that Ingrid had to look away.

She asked if they wanted something to eat.

Father and son said no, thank you, they had brought some food with them, but Adolf wanted a word with her and seemed to have to pluck up the courage before he was able to stutter that he had her færing in his boat shed, he didn't know if she wanted it back or perhaps rather *when* she wanted it back.

Ingrid screwed up her eyes and said she didn't know, either. What did he think?

"I thought perhaps not just yet," Adolf said.

Ingrid didn't react.

Adolf from Malvika had been the island's anchor on the mainland for all these years, now he gave a few thoughtful nods, and said he just thought he ought to mention it, that was all, no, there was something else, he pulled a folded sheet of paper from his shirt pocket and passed it to her. Ingrid read her own handwriting, a plea to all kind people to help this man, who must never be allowed to die, that was how she had expressed herself.

She swung the plait behind her back, she had only one now, and looked at the old man as if he had been trespassing on her island. He glanced nervously at his son and said he just wanted her to know.

"Know what?"

"That everything's fine."

He said goodbye with a bow, strode over to his boat and

muttered something to his son about the sail. Ingrid pushed the boat out and waited until they had hoisted the sail, until the wind had caught it and Adolf had settled in the stern with the tiller under his arm. Daniel waved.

Barbro led the ewe up to the barn and Ingrid carried the sack of flour. They put the pail of milk in the larder and Barbro continued to cry tears of joy and told Ingrid how hellish it had been at the hospital, the food, the nurses, the doctors . . . While Ingrid sat in the rocking chair listening to the sound of another person talking, missed her cat, Koshka, she was still holding the sheet of paper and wondered why he had given it to the very first person he encountered.

Because he couldn't read it? Because he didn't trust her? And how many other reasons were there?

Barbro clattered the pans on the stove rings, jerked the pump handle up and down and slopped about and threw out the fish guts that had been left in the bowl in the larder, had Ingrid bin s' out o' he' wits that she'd gutted 'em in th' house?

She started cooking. Ingrid folded the sheet of paper and had to say something, she said they didn't have any fodder for the sheep.

Barbro said it could feed on the old grass now that the snow had gone, they hadn't mown it in the summer, they could boil up some cattle feed from kelp and fish-heads, let it graze on seaweed, they could *buy* hay.

And they had some straw in the barn on Gjesøya, Ingrid said, and Barbro took a break from her big homecoming clean-up, a concerned furrow appeared between her eyebrows, as she said:

"Bi God tha's changed."

"Hvur . . . ?"

"Tha's got comely."

Ingrid was about to say she always had been, but her aunt stood weighing her up with the same bend of the hip, as if she couldn't believe it. Barbro went right up to her, grabbed the plait and studied it, tossed it back and returned to the pots and pans humming maddeningly – and Ingrid, in her agitation, remembered where she had hidden her sketch pad: she had run up to the closet as soon as she had seen the men in the boat, taken the pad and dashed around the house in panic until she found a less safe place, fool that she was: under the mattress in her grandfather's bed. But Barbro stood in front of her like a wall, with the potato bucket dangling from her little finger, still wearing that same irritating smile.

Ingrid grabbed the bucket and went out into the rain, opened the cellar door and knelt down to let the light in, picked potatoes like eggs from a nest and stacked them in circles, counted them and was sure beyond all doubt that she was right about it, then she went in and put the bucket on the worktop next to the sink, continued into her grandfather's room, whisked the bedding aside to make sure the pad really was there, and it was.

She clutched it to her bosom, opened it and saw again the fir cones and shells from her schooldays, the Russian poem consisting of three unreadable verses of three identical lines, shifted from one foot to the other and rocked up and down, until she no longer had any doubt she had the pad in her arms, then she went to the loft and slipped it under the bed linen in the closet where it belonged, in the North Chamber.

When she was on her way down again, Barbro was standing at the bottom of the stairs with her hands on her hips, and asked:

"Hvo's the feither?"

Ingrid descended the last steps, swept her aside, continued into the kitchen and said several times – it sounded like a litany – that it was none of Barbro's business, what the hell did it have to do with her who the father was, then changed tack completely and reluctantly admitted something about a whaler from Reine, and Barbro stood there looking as if she was searching for a reason to doubt her.

She asked what his name was.

Ingrid didn't answer. Barbro nodded, alreit then, turned and lifted a chunk of fish from the water and waited for Ingrid to come alongside so that they could admire the rainbow sheen on the gleaming white flesh and work together to find that delicate balance between well-cooked and overcooked fish. Barbro asked where she had caught it. Ingrid said near Skogsholmen, as far as she could remember, she wasn't sure.

"Wi' a hand lein?"

"Ya . . ."

Barbro looked at her.

Ingrid asked whether they shouldn't just forget about the

liver, fry the fish in margarine, now Barbro was home again with her coupons and they had double rations, they could celebrate, couldn't they?

Barbro said she wanted liver, she hadn't had any for years and a day, and they should eat off the porcelain plates and drink redcurrant juice.

Ingrid said there wasn't any more redcurrant juice.

Barbro said that wasn't possible with all the juicing and preserving they had done in the summer.

Ingrid said the jars had burst in the frost while she was away.

Barbro asked where she had been.

Ingrid said she had been working at the trading post.

Barbro turned to face her and asked if there had been anyone on the island all the autumn. Ingrid said no and knew that her sketch pad had not only come to light, to her suffocating relief, but had brought along with it the onset of a new darkness.

She went outside and stared up at the falling rain.

On her return, she saw her aunt had set the table.

Ingrid dried herself, and they ate in silence, apart from Barbro praising the food and singing both before and after the meal. Ingrid did not comment on her singing.

Then they wrapped up, went out and fetched a spike and a rope tied to an iron ring, led the sheep into the nearest garden, hammered the spike into the ground and placed the ring over it, watched until the animal began to nibble at the brown blades of grass. Then they walked home.

They did some housework, went down again and moved the

spike. Barbro said it wasn't necessary to have the sheep tethered, there was nowhere for it to go.

Ingrid said now at least it wouldn't jump into the sea.

They laughed at that.

When night fell they went and led it back to the barn and gave it a tuft of dry hay. This was the most important sheep they had ever had; had it not been a sheep they would have kept it in the house.

# 4

In February the sea is turquoise and the islands are as white as mountaintops. But they have dark edges. The sky is as hard as ice, and Ingrid doesn't row over to the village, she heads for Stangholmen instead, where old Thomas sells her all the hay she wants. She sits at the side of his wife, Inga, who is bedridden, talking island language and drinking coffee substitute.

Inga, too, can see the circumstances Ingrid is in, but refrains from asking whether the child has a father. Ingrid asks how she knows, as it doesn't show. Inga smiles. She tells her that dead bodies have also been washed ashore on Stangholmen, they were picked up by the Germans with the cargo boat. But she doesn't know any more about the disaster, nor has there been anything about it in the paper Thomas occasionally brings with him.

Ingrid loads the hay onto her boat and rows home.

The following week she is back. Now Inga is on her feet again and says "Well, A cheited th' Reaper this teim, too". They help Ingrid to load the hay into the boat, and they don't ask whether the child has a father this time, either. But when

Thomas has gone inside the house, Ingrid asks Inga how premature a baby can be and still survive? Inga says that was a strange question, but two of her own were premature, the first by two whole months, as far as she could work out.

"An' she's hier yet."

And so February passes, without Ingrid rowing over to the trading post, Barbro does instead.

Ingrid is sitting with the sheep, suspecting that her aunt is up to something, and also hoping it will lead somewhere – *something* has to happen at some point. And when Barbro returns late in the afternoon, she searches her face, without discerning anything, except that her aunt has had a spot of bother with Margot, the same old story, did Margot have any news, Ingrid asks.

"Leik hva?" Barbro snaps.

Ingrid asks if she has spoken to anyone else. Barbro says yes, to the Lensmann.

"Henriksen?"

Barbro is being secretive, and she never looks more stupid than when she has a secret. Ingrid says he isn't a lensmann now.

Barbro says she knows.

Ingrid asks if she saw any soldiers or military vehicles?

Barbro no longer looks stupid.

"The' r' all in th' Fort," she says, and informs Ingrid that Barrøy will have to house some of the refugees from Finnmark, that is what Henriksen had told her, he would be coming over one of these days to get Ingrid's signature, it is Ingrid's island.

Ingrid says that the two of them should decide about that and asks whether Barbro got hold of a cat at Jenny and Hanna's. Barbro says she forgot.

Ingrid says she forgets so many things nowadays, it is probably her age, and goes out to find something to busy herself with, such as clearing out the Swedes' quay house, where she sees the physical reminders of so many lives that are no more that it is a trial to carry them through the snow to the old Lofoten boat shed, which has been closed off for such a long time that everything in there is also a physical reminder of something that is no more. In the course of the day she discovers even more. But a new order has been created – in the Swedes' quay house at least.

She goes back home and sits in the kitchen watching Barbro cooking. After they have eaten Barbro sets about making nets. Ingrid falls asleep in the rocking chair and is woken by the sound of her aunt clattering pots and pans on the stove. She feels saliva running down her chin. Barbro tells her to carry on sleeping, being in the condition she is. Ingrid counts how many meshes her aunt has made in the netting, goes up to the loft and lies down, but can't sleep.

Henriksen didn't arrive as he did previously, with a requisitioned cargo boat and a troop of soldiers, but alone, in his old motorised tub, he moored at the quay and just managed to claw his way ashore.

Ingrid and Barbro stood at the kitchen window watching

him struggle up to the house through the snowdrifts. Barbro wanted to go out and help him, but Ingrid held her back and let him come right up to the porch and knock on the door, before she said come in, in the quietest of voices.

He came in, took off his fur cap and mittens, closed the door and stared into space, with eyes like two boils in a red, swollen face which had become completely ravaged since Ingrid last saw him, she was on the point of asking him to take a seat.

Barbro told him to take a seat and asked if he would like some coffee.

He lowered himself onto the nearest chair and groaned yes, without looking at Ingrid.

She asked why he had come alone, there were three of them on the Board, weren't there?

He looked as if he thought that might be a barbed question, glanced out at the snow on the window ledge and said nothing until the silence became unbearable, twisted his stiff body into position and mumbled in a barely audible voice that they had decided the Barrøy islanders would have to take the Hætta family from Finnmark, a mother and four children who had been quartered at the rectory, they were destroying the furniture there, breaking cups and glasses, and the Board didn't want to be held responsible for this, next week a new load of refugees would be arriving, there was no end to this bloody war.

Ingrid gave an uncomfortable laugh and said the Hætta family should stay where they were. Barbro, who was standing with the coffee pot in her hand, turned and looked at her in surprise.

"But the' ca' bi hier, can't the'?"

"No, the' can't bi hier," Ingrid shouted, losing her composure.

"Hvafor not?"

"Hvar's th' money? Hvur ar' we goen' t' feed 'em?"

Barbro shook her head, put the cups on the table, poured the coffee and muttered something incomprehensible as she went back and banged the coffee pot down on the stove.

"The girl needs to go to school," Ingrid said flatly.

Henriksen blew on the coffee, looked around for some sugar, gave up, poured the coffee into the saucer and began to slurp, wiped his mouth with the back of his hand and said it was the Board that made the decisions, Ingrid had to comply.

"No," Ingrid said.

For the first time he looked directly at her, but instead of losing his temper he fell into a reverie, and Ingrid couldn't decide whether she was watching a display of a guilty man's shame-filled repentance in those infected eyes of his, or yet another manifestation of dotage, or war, as if Henriksen, too, had been stricken by it.

"We can take the three lads from Hammerfest," she said. "Or Skarsvåg. The ones that are in Molandsvika."

Now he looked even more surprised. "They know how to handle the boats," she continued. "And fish. They can work."

"But they have to go to school, too."

Ingrid said nothing.

Henriksen sipped his coffee, looking as though he had just won a major victory, leaned forwards with a self-important grunt, then fished out a creased document and placed it on the table between them. Ingrid recognised the form and read that the Board had found Barrøy suitable as a place of temporary residence for between five and eight persons . . . all whilst wondering how she could elicit from him – without asking outright – what exactly had happened here when he came with Hargel before Christmas, what they had done to her.

Henriksen conceded that the three young men might not be so happy in Molandsvika, although who the hell was in these times.

Ingrid asked what was wrong with the times.

He shouted that he had never been able to work her out, the bitch.

Ingrid asked where the Leutnant was, Hargel.

Henriksen first answered the question – in the Fort on Nordøya – then said, what sort of a question was that, for Christ's sake!

Ingrid told him to clear off, an' don't show tha face hier again.

Barbro smacked the coffee pot down on the stove once more. Henriksen got up shaking his head so violently that it looked as if it was about to fall off, swept his mittens and fur cap from the table with an angry flourish and strode out of the door, still cursing. Ingrid kept screaming at him until he had passed the window and they could see the black figure battling his way down through the snow, ponderous and heavy-legged. Far too long after that they heard the drone of a distant engine, short, sharp heartbeats, then they were gone, too.

Barbro managed to get Ingrid down into the rocking chair, war she *heill* barkers? Ingrid felt a cool hand stroke her lower arm and began to recount what had happened in the winter, aware with every word that passed her lips that it became more horrific than it had been, but also different, as though it was about somebody else, not herself, and that she was beginning to talk to herself, as an islander must in order not to go to pieces, until her voice dropped and everything faded into a long silence – the two or three days *before* the men came had also gone, the days from the night *he* left her until *they* found her; she didn't know *when* the darkness set in, whether it was brought on by him or herself, or by the loss of that which could not disappear from her mind.

Something had happened to Barbro's face while Ingrid was talking, something Ingrid had never seen before, but had nonetheless sensed must have been there, since she wasn't surprised to discover it, it was as if Barbro, too, could have secrets, and had the ability to keep them. Ingrid placed a hand on her arm and her aunt shook it off. Ingrid went out into the barn that evening as well, and sat with the sheep.

# 5

At the crack of dawn next day Barbro rowed to the village, without saying a word before she left, and returned late in the afternoon with provisions, apparently the same person she had always been, but saying excitedly that they had to go over in two days and accompany Margot's son to the Fort, where he was to pick up a steelyard.

Ingrid said she had never heard the like of it.

"A *steelyard*?!"

Yes, that was as much as Barbro knew, Margot was going to slaughter some animals and needed the heavy-duty scales she had lent the Germans . . .

"Hva? Slachter 'em *nu*?" Ingrid screamed, out of herself.

"Ya, she's run out o'*fodder*," Barbro yelled defiantly at the ceiling beams – wasn't Ingrid going to do anything today, either, they were supposed to be doing some baking, weren't they?

Ingrid went out and considered rowing to Stangholmen again to talk to Inga, or putting out some nets, instead though she threw up, looked down at the vomit and wondered what she had eaten, rooted around in it with her fingers, as if searching for some lost memory, until she felt stupid and went in and washed and started rolling *lefse* dough into perfectly round cakes as her tears flowed and neither of them spoke.

"Ca' tha cope?" Barbro said before they went to bed.

"Yes, I can," Ingrid said.

They got up before daybreak, gave the sheep a full ration of cow fodder and rowed to the village. Margot's son, Markus, wasn't old enough to drive a small lorry, but did so anyway, he transported barrels of herring, sacks of flour and supplies as well as people to the military camps on the main island.

Ingrid and Barbro sat on the back with Jenny and three other women who had various complaints to present: one of them had an issue with Henriksen's Board, a second wanted the Germans to give back the boat they had requisitioned from her husband, or at least to let him "borrow" it for the spring. Ingrid didn't find out what Jenny was after, she was silent, she was in Barbro's hands.

An army of vacant-eyed, brown-clad figures was streaming through the camp gates as they arrived, Russian prisoners of war on their way to work on the roads. Behind them five half-cylinders of corrugated iron stretched out over the ground like gigantic ridges between furrows in a field, beneath the virgin snow that had melted along their tops. In front of the telegraph office stood a green jeep with the Red Cross symbol on the bonnet and doors, spewing grey exhaust fumes into the cold.

Markus waited until the column had passed, got out and struck up a conversation with a uniformed soldier. They discussed, pointed and clearly came to some agreement. Markus returned and shouted that the women should get down from the back of the lorry and follow him.

They walked in single file down towards a massive block of ice, which in fact was a concrete bunker, where Markus came to a halt in front of an unpainted door and knocked twice and waited until a soldier stuck his head out and asked in broken Norwegian what they wanted. Markus said something about the scales, the steelyard, he had been promised he would have it today, but said nothing about the women.

Jenny screamed that they wanted to talk to Hargel, he was a good man.

The soldier considered the request and opened the door.

Inside there was electricity, from a roaring diesel generator, but it was so dark that it took time for their eyes to adjust from the snow to the artificial tawny glow. Two doors were open, one in each end-wall, a line of prisoners with bowed heads came through the first and passed a table littered with a typewriter, handguns and helmets, a telephone and untidy piles of papers. Beside it stood the biggest steelyard on the island, as well as Leutnant Albert Emil Hargel and a Red Cross soldier. On the platform of the scales sat four prisoners squeezed together, their bony knees under their chins. Hargel slid the counterweights along the arm, found the balancing point and called out:

*"Zweihundertvierzig Kilo!"*

The Red Cross soldier noted it down and divided the number by four in a loud voice, was met with a "*Ja, ungefähr*", thereabouts, from the Leutnant, who a moment later noticed Markus and signalled to him to come closer.

"Russian flab," he said with a broad grin and shifted the weights to the left so that the platform hit the floor. The prisoners struggled to their feet and disappeared through the second door in a straggly line. Four new prisoners were called forward and squeezed onto the scales. Hargel repeated the process with the weights.

*"Zweihundertzweiundzwanzig."*

He leaned forwards and said something to the soldier, who nodded and turned to Jenny, who was first in the queue, and asked what the ladies wanted.

The one who wanted to have her husband's boat returned presented her case in such a strident voice that Ingrid had to look away. The soldier gave a faint smile and translated.

Hargel, with his back to her, said in German:

"O.K., O.K., just take it."

Then he appeared to remember something that irritated him, turned and caught sight of Ingrid.

*"Ah, die Inselbewohnerin, geht es Ihnen besser?"*

The interpreter asked Ingrid if she was better, and she said twice that she was doing fine and asked the interpreter – without looking at Hargel – whether they had found out any more about the body in her barn.

The interpreter didn't understand, she repeated the question, stumbling over her words, while Hargel followed with interest. The interpreter decided on a translation. Which took time to articulate. Hargel understood what he was getting at, shook his head and said:

"*Ne ne, auch Russe.*"

Then muttered something the interpreter translated, telling her that the man had been a Russian P.O.W., not a German officer, and Ingrid felt she was getting warmer, but not warm enough, and asked in a mumble whether there had been any Germans on board?

"*An bord – wo?*"

"On the *Rigel.*"

"*Ja, sicher, viele.*" Lots of them.

"How many?" Ingrid ventured in broken German.

"How should I know? *Viele!* Isn't that good enough for you?"

Ingrid braced herself and asked why they had beaten her. The interpreter answered angrily, off his own bat, that hiding survivors from the *Rigel* was punishable by death, no matter whether they were deserters, Russians or Norwegians.

"Deserters?"

Barbro took a step forward and bellowed:

"Ingrid wants t' know if thi fucked 'er."

A gasp ran through the assembly, the interpreter blushed and barked at her to shut her mouth. Barbro didn't move. She repeated what she had said, and the interpreter repeated his command with a snarl as Hargel glanced enquiringly from one to the other. The interpreter turned to him and whispered in his ear, as if sharing a confidence. Hargel's face lit up and he turned to Ingrid.

"Ah, you're pregnant? My warmest congratulations."

Ingrid was taken aback. Then she burst into laughter. Hargel's smile faded into something resembling concern, he folded his arms, was there anything else?

Ingrid said no.

He shook his head and said:

"*Schöne Frau*, why do you always go around in those rags?"

The interpreter muttered in Norwegian:

"Not important."

And announced to the crowd: "Keep it short. This is a military camp, not a tribunal. Next."

The woman wanting to complain about Henriksen shouted that the Rations and Relocation Board had filled her house with refugees she had neither the space nor food for, she had three small kids and an ageing mother to take care of, and her husband was in Lofoten.

Hargel's distant, guttural voice:

"*Mein Gott.*"

Ingrid watched as silent, emaciated prisoners, four at a time, squeezed onto a meat scale to prove officially that they weren't dead, heard a considerable number of kilos in German being divided by four, smelled wet straw, sweat, diesel, cowshed and rotten herring as winter bore down on them through the open doors. Money was handed over and the steelyard was carried into the swirling snow by two prisoners and loaded onto the back of the lorry. Ingrid clambered up, sat beside Barbro, with her back to the cab, and placed her mittens over her invisible belly.

Ingrid had been here before, accompanying her father, with a borrowed horse and cart, *her* on the horse and him in the cart, his voice, could she see anything around the next bend, could they get through?

She was his lookout, her fingers gripping the stiff, white mane hard, the creaking shafts and the slapping of the straps against the horse's sweaty hindquarters, a summer that dissolved into white smoke when Barbro shouted in her ear that it war divilish cold.

Ingrid saw herself walking down to the dory at the landing stage through a veil of dry snow, led like a lamb to slaughter between Hargel and Henriksen, with a blanket over her shoulders, sobbing and shaking, and being shipped on a December day over to the trading post, where Jenny was summoned, Jenny, who the following morning took her on board the steamer, where she was cared for by another woman; the damp heat of the smoke-filled lounge, the first encounter with Dr Erik Falc Johannesen, who held his head at an odd angle and showed no interest in her at all until she took off three layers of clothing and refused to speak.

Why didn't she speak?

Ingrid wondered if they were her own clothes.

Then she saw that the woman who accompanied her was Eva Sofie, who had been down south to collect two other patients: Eva Sofie had held her hand in the lounge on the steamer, had slept in the same cabin as her, given her fish balls in a white curry sauce and floury potatoes with red skins, thickly piled open sandwiches, the smell of fried onions, the engine shaking every bolt in the hull . . . Eva Sofie had known Ingrid for five weeks, Ingrid had known *her* for three.

She wanted to get to her feet on the back of the lorry, but Barbro held her down – and Ingrid heard Hargel and Henriksen arguing about whether she was worth sparing as she wouldn't tell them anything, Hargel had eventually lost his temper and hit Henriksen on the cheekbone with his black rubber cosh, Hargel had saved her life.

Ingrid asked Jenny why she hadn't given her some decent clothes to wear before she put her on board the steamer, just before Christmas. Jenny smiled:

"We couldn't git th' clout off tha, doesn't tha remember?"

Yes, she did. Ingrid remembered, but:

"War the' mine?"

"Ya . . ."

"Hvur did A look?"

"Not a pretty seit, the' must a thrash'd tha . . ."

Eva Sofie got her down the icy gangplank in the unfamiliar town and into the vehicle that took her to the hospital, where, with two others, whom she still couldn't see, she was registered under her correct name, which she spelled out herself, before being led into a hot shower and afterwards put between white sheets, the others were Ada and Signy, the two old women with the same grey hair, they, too, had been stricken by the war.

# 6

They stood outside the store watching the scales being carried in by Markus and two counter-jumpers. The other women said goodbye and went their separate ways. Ingrid stayed where she was and looked around. Barbro eyed her, wondering. Ingrid said:

"A have t' write a letter."

"Has tha . . . ?"

They walked up the hill to the rectory and were brushing the snow off each other in the hallway when the kitchen door opened and Sara stuck her head out, recognised Ingrid and ran back in, shouting.

The kitchen was a mess. Ingrid said My God and Barbro said Th' Divil teik me. Anja was pleased to see them and hugged Ingrid and glanced searchingly up at her, as if to assure herself that she was in one of her stable moods.

Ingrid pulled herself free and enquired about Mikkel, who had fled under the table and refused to come out, and about Ante, whom she spotted through the door to the drawing room, where he was sitting on the floor with half a porcelain cup in his mouth. Nelvy and Gunvor were each on a chair eating leftovers with their fingers, Nelvy in the old red woollen hat pulled down over her ears, with short, brown tufts sticking out through two holes.

Ingrid asked why they weren't at school and was told that the teacher was ill. She drilled her eyes into Anja, who shrugged. Barbro bent down and looked at Mikkel and asked what he was doing under the table. He covered his face with his hands. Then Ellen came running in and wanted to sit on Ingrid's lap. Ingrid had slumped down onto the wood bin. Ellen asked her if she had any cakes.

"But you've got food," Ingrid said, nodding towards the plates on the table, put Ellen down again and said she should come with her to write some letters, whereupon she went into the study, where beds had been made up on the two leather sofas. She asked who was sleeping there. Sara came in and said it was her and Ellen, their room was too cold.

Ingrid asked if they knew how to make coffee. They looked at each other. She told them to go and ask their mother to make some. They ran out. Ingrid sat at the priest's desk, found some paper, a pen and ink, and wrote Dear Eva Sofie, she had arrived safe and sound and was now in the fortunate position of being able to thank her for all the things she could now remember, the food on the steamer, the writing on the wall and Eva Sofie's unstinting patience, it was Ada and Signy they had been with on the boat, wasn't it?

Say hello to them.

And to the doctor, Erik Falc.

Ingrid would never forget any of them, she didn't forget things anymore, but there was still the question of the clothes, whether they were hers, and what's more whether they were torn when Eva Sofie took charge of her. And even if she could assume that Hargel hadn't used force, there was still the matter of Henriksen's festering eyes.

She put the letter in an envelope, found some stamps, went into the kitchen and drank the coffee standing while chatting to Barbro about the weather and how much hay they had given the sheep.

They decided to spend the night at the rectory, and Ingrid went down to Margot's with the letter.

They made dinner and cleaned the rooms in turn together with Anja and Johanna Matea and the other mother. The two men had moved out and were sleeping at the trading post. Ingrid asked Johanna Matea why she didn't light the fire in the girls' room. Johanna Matea said she had been ordered by Henriksen to save fuel. Ingrid remonstrated that the shed was full of wood, and nobody had touched the coke bin all winter, she should light the fire in all the rooms.

Johanna Matea looked unsure.

Ingrid said if she didn't do as she said she would take the keys from her and throw her out. Johanna Matea said, alright then, but the girls would have to bring in the coke and light the fires themselves, and her nipper had a rash, could Ingrid have a look at him?

Ingrid was shown a well-fed boy with plump red cheeks, six months old or thereabouts, she felt his pulse, noted that he didn't have a temperature and eased him into Barbro's arms. Barbro pinched his cheek, he opened his eyes and screamed, and she said that if there was anything wrong with him, it was that he was too tubby.

The children laughed.

Johanna Matea didn't. Ingrid asked if Henriksen often made an appearance. Johanna Matea didn't reply, in a way that indicated he was often there. Ingrid asked whether he was bothering her. Johanna Matea looked away and still said nothing as clearly as possible. Ingrid said she shouldn't put up with it. Johanna Matea said that was easy for her to say. No, Ingrid said, he was a dirty old pig, she didn't owe him a thing, she should lock both doors at night. Johanna Matea said they weren't allowed to lock the doors. Ingrid repeated her threat to throw her out if she didn't do as she said. Johanna Matea looked as if she were about to cry, but changed her mind and found some matter to attend to, with her back turned to Ingrid.

Ingrid took Nelvy into the drawing room and asked to feel her head. Nelvy looked as though she had been expecting something like this and took off her hat without prompting. Ingrid felt the strange bumps beneath the new, thick hair, which made them less visible, and said that Nelvy had a fine head of hair and didn't need to wear a hat, and certainly not indoors. Nelvy asked why her head wasn't nice and round like the other children's. Ingrid said she didn't know, but a head can be as bumpy as it wants, as long as you let your hair grow and make sure it is clean so that it doesn't rot and fall out beneath a dirty hat.

Nelvy gave this some thought.

Ingrid asked if her head hurt.

Nelvy said no.

Ingrid found a woollen thread, tied a bow around a lock of hair and told Nelvy to go and look in the large hallway mirror. Nelvy went and gazed at herself in the mirror and came back. Ingrid asked what she thought. Nelvy said it looked nice.

They went back to the kitchen and Ingrid asked Barbro to sing. Barbro was shy and said Ingrid had never asked her to do that before. Ingrid looked at her in surprise. No, Barbro wasn't going to sing. But Sara said yes, yes, and the others nodded. Barbro turned her back on them and sang in such a way that nobody knew what to do when the song was over. Johanna Matea looked around, wide-eyed with disbelief, and said they should clap. Barbro grabbed a towel and said, no, they shouldn't. They clapped all the same, Barbro blushed and Nelvy didn't put her hat back on.

Ingrid and Barbro removed the bed linen from the study, scrubbed the two rooms where the men had slept too, and spent the night at the rectory.

Next morning Ingrid took the children to school, discovered that the teacher was indeed ill, returned in a cheery mood and told Johanna Matea she would come every week to see how they were doing, and immediately noticed that there was something wrong, something she couldn't see, but feel, which was not dissimilar to what had happened on Barrøy that winter, and she asked Nelvy if she wanted to go to the island with her.

Anja and Johanna Matea thought this a strange question, had Ingrid been given permission by the Board?

Nelvy said yes.

There was a little argument regarding who got what from the sack she shared with Gunvor, but Ingrid said there were plenty of clothes on the island, nice ones too, as long as she had enough to keep her warm on the boat when they rowed over. Nelvy asked if Gunvor could come, too. Ingrid said yes. But Gunvor wanted to stay with Sara, and Nelvy didn't seem to mind.

Ingrid wondered whether to hold her hand as they walked down to buy provisions. Nelvy settled the question by taking Ingrid's hand and not letting go, not even when they were at the counter talking to Margot who, after they had made their purchases, began to whisper and make faces, which caused Ingrid to ask her to speak up.

Margot made more faces and told Ingrid to come with her into the stockroom. Ingrid slipped Nelvy's hand into Barbro's, followed her in and was told in a whisper to spend all her money as quickly as possible, the money Margot somehow knew she had received from Malmberget, the priest, because something was about to happen, she had heard it from her son, Markus, he not only delivered goods to the Fort, he also had a radio, and if everything goes to the wall, money is worthless.

Ingrid hesitated.

Margot's bosom swelled and heaved mightily, she hissed that Ingrid had caused a lot of trouble over the years, but she warn't no cod-head.

Ingrid didn't know whether she was being tricked or being given an unwarranted piece of good advice, for some unknown reason, but she was in no hurry to find out. She turned and walked out of the store with Margot's voice ringing in her ears:

"They're goen' t' teik ev'rythin', an' mind it war me that told tha!"

Ingrid and Nelvy walked down to the boat and rowed back in softly falling snow, Ingrid realised that once again she had forgotten the cat – and laughed, because now they had Nelvy. When they were home they gave the sheep some fodder, set up Nelvy in Ingrid's old bedroom and showed her the new clothes and her things, it took all day, and in the evening they put out some nets, two lengths.

# 7

March is the month of the year for which there is least use. The islanders see the sun rise and are deceived by the light, which only makes the winter more apparent. And April is equally insidious and even more treacherous. But the Eurasian oyster-catchers come anyway, and create their din, there are sounds in the sky and on the rocks, one layer of headscarves and socks can be removed, the enormous sheep wanders around the brown gardens nibbling at old grass as the snowstorms continue to swirl, just as hope threatens to call forth a smile or two in the human spirit; the islanders both curse and freeze more than they did in January, but they remove another headscarf all the same, they are *urging* spring to come.

A few fish as well have appeared on the rack where the P.O.W. uniforms hung in the winter. The three Skarsvåg brothers have put them there, and Ingrid can feel how this everyday sight has superimposed itself upon the old one without erasing it, *this* too is a clock, a passing of time, which points forwards, and might go her way.

The brothers come to the island at the beginning of March and are accommodated in the Swedes' quay house. They have their own stove, eat all their meals in the main house and inherit their clothes from the male population that is no longer there. But even though they have grown up beside an even wilder sea than the one Ingrid and Barbro have access to, they are both carpenters and children and need time to familiarise themselves with boats and fishing gear and everything else that sets Barrøy apart from what they know. They have good sea legs, learn quickly and never feel the cold.

At the start Ingrid is with them to say where the nets should be, and the lines, which Barbro teaches them to mend and bait. And Arne, the one with the dead eye, knows how to squeeze the utmost out of his two younger brothers, telling them that if they can stick it out, one day he will take them back to Hammerfest.

Both Sverre and Helmer consider their home to be Skarsvåg, Hammerfest is only where their parents are buried.

Yes, but do they remember Skarsvåg at all?

Of course they do.

How well, though?

Arne refreshes their memories, of neighbours and relatives and steep, black mountains that are green at the bottom in the summer time. But he still thinks his words arouse insufficient interest, so he glances across at Ingrid, who says they can stay on Barrøy for as long as they like, now she is going to follow Margot's advice and spend the rest of her money on a pile of planks that have lain behind the trading post for a number of years, pending an extension out towards the canning factory, an extension which will never come to anything, knowing the foreman. He has said no to her request twice, but Ingrid knows that one day he is going to say yes, and that this day is fast approaching – she will rebuild the houses in Karvika, convert the ruins into homes, banish the fear and superstition and finally write the letter to her cousin Lars in Lofoten asking him to return, the letter that should have been written so long ago that she has forgotten where her resistance came from, the type of forgetfulness that even an Eric Falc can appreciate, Ingrid is beginning to take risks, which is also one aspect of losing control.

One fine day she and Arne row to Malvika to collect the færing from Adolf, and on the way back Arne asks whether he and his brothers will be paid for their work on Barrøy, in Molandsvika they weren't given a penny, and barely any food.

Ingrid notes that it has taken him close on a month to bring this matter up. She laughs and says, we will all be paid one day, they are going to sell the fish as early as possible this year, hopefully before it is too late, she has been in Margot's stockroom and has seen it is crammed full of goods, which presumably are a much stronger currency than money in times like these.

Arne and his brothers will get what they are due.

Then they will collect eggs and sell them too, and eider down, but as usual it won't be sold for a year or ten, hopefully at the very moment they can get almost as much for it as it is worth. Ingrid's father knew the price of a finished eiderdown, now Ingrid does too, and never on this earth has there been less equivalence between what a commodity costs and what those who create it receive.

Arne understands this.

Ingrid asks him what his plans are.

Arne is rowing hard and doesn't want to go into detail, there is something evasive about him, but one thing is sure, they are going back to Finnmark.

His eye is no longer a red beacon, but a piece of matt glass Ingrid has learned how to read. She says there is nothing in Finnmark. He says that if it is as she claims, with regard to money, then that might mean the war will soon be over and then whatever is in ruins now can be rebuilt.

Ingrid says all that about the war ending now is no more than wishful thinking.

"O.K.," Arne says, continuing to row with his massive arms, and it occurs to Ingrid to ask him when the brothers' birthdays are. He asks her why she wants to know. No reason, Ingrid says.

Before they arrive on Barrøy she also contrives to ask Arne if he is ready to take on the work of rebuilding the houses in Karvika, after all he is a carpenter, he will get paid for that too, she says.

He asks:

"With money that is worthless?"

Ingrid laughs.

*

But she doesn't laugh often this spring, and never out loud, because in the person of Nelvy they have taken a quiet, enigmatic creature into their home. She stays there not only for the first week – she is silent and hard to fathom, even though she holds Ingrid's hand and answers no when asked whether she misses Gunvor. She stays on the island because Ingrid cannot bring herself to send her back to the rectory when school starts again, for the same inexplicable reasons that made her bring her to Barrøy.

Nelvy's hair grows and is thick and attractive. Ingrid washes and combs and twists it into small plaits. She no longer wears a hat, but a headscarf. Her lips are dainty and her teeth white and nicely regular, and she has two blue lumps on the sides of her nose that become more pronounced with every day that passes, even though Ingrid does her best to ignore them.

Barbro says there is something strange about the girl.

Ingrid says she is as she is; to herself she says she is exactly like *me*, can't you see that, you daft thing?

They set the hands of the repaired wall-clock at random, to three, for example, and read Ingrid's old school books until it is four o'clock; they practise writing the alphabet until it is five, and draw shells, which Ingrid says are the finest on the island; they collect them, too, although, strangely, they have no value at all, indeed there is hardly anything on the island that has less value, even Nelvy thinks this is weird.

She eats a little less than they would like her to, but says she loves Barbro's cooking, she repairs the eider houses with Ingrid and helps to split and tail-tie the fish the Finnmark boys bring ashore and gut and hang. But she is best at it when someone helps her. And although she is making progress with numbers, letters and words, Ingrid feels she reacts to too many questions – such as does she remember her parents or anything of the journey from Kirkenes to Hammerfest? – by wanting to go and lie down, even though it might be the middle of the day. And Ingrid regards it as a form of laziness, which doesn't make her angry but weary, at a time when there is no room for more weariness, for although Ingrid can endure more and more of what is still coming back to her, she has now received a letter from Eva Sofie. It informs her that her clothes were intact when she arrived, as far as she can recall, who can recall that sort of thing, and this is not the definitive answer that Ingrid had been hoping for, while the blue lumps around Nelvy's nose are becoming more and more prominent as the spring fails to appear.

Ingrid wonders whether to put Nelvy in her own bed in the North Chamber so that she can keep an eye on her round the clock and whether she should take her to see a doctor, but she puts off making any decision.

The eider ducks waddle onto land, the black-backed gulls lay their first eggs, which Ingrid and Nelvy test in buckets of water and cover with sand in half-barrels, and these are followed by the smaller gulls. Nelvy enjoys this work, the warm eggs in her hand, and Ingrid has to keep taking her head in her hands, feeling for the lumps and hoping they will soon go.

One day Nelvy says that her parents are dead.

Ingrid doesn't know what to answer, she asks how Nelvy can know, and Nelvy mounts a weak smile. They make three new eider houses from sheets of slate they collect from the beach in the west and brush clean, two form the walls and one is placed on top as a roof. Then they cover them with peat and fill them with some of last year's hay, and the following morning they find Nelvy dead in bed.

Ingrid lies down beside her and stays there until she is cold, and she doesn't hear Barbro, who comes in and tries to drag her out of bed and shouts, it stinks hier, th' girl has messed herself.

Ingrid has experienced this before, not being able to live after someone has died. She gets up later that evening, shoos the others out, carries Nelvy down and washes her in the kitchen, the child's white body with no lumps, and dresses her in the finest clothes she herself wore when she was a child. Arne and his brothers spend the night making a coffin and Nelvy lies on two trestles in the boat shed until they bury her beside Ingrid's grandparents in the cemetery by the sea, even though there isn't a priest in the village; an old sea captain from Finnmark does the honours.

His name is Lukas Wara and in the bright sunlight, which for some reason is shining that day, he holds forth on bounteous mercy and the bane of life, and what is more he also has a pious cough.

They consider writing Nelvy Barrøy on the cross, for it turns out that Arvola is not Nelvy's family name but Gunvor's, and in Henriksen's papers no surname for Nelvy has been entered, but in the end they decide not to. They don't have a date of birth either, so they also omit the date of death, leaving only Here rests Nelvy in foreign soil, and the year she died.

Nelvy too was a victim of the war, there can be no doubt about that, and those standing silent around the coffin are overcome more by profound anguish than tears, with the exception of Helmer, who is crying like a human being, the boy who used to tease Nelvy because she couldn't tail-tie fish. But this may also have something to do with their being more or less the same age and coming from the same county, a county that is no more, which Captain Wara also mentions; he is from the town of Vadsø by Varanger Fjord, where Finns and Norwegians have lived side by side for hundreds of years, he himself has roots in both peoples and he says he knows only one Greek word, which startles the others as they were expecting a Finnish one, however it is the most important word of all, it is *angelos*, which means angel, and he finishes by saying that the depressing memory of the destruction of Finnmark will follow Nelvy down into the grave and on into heaven. The others console Helmer, who hides behind his brothers and wants none of this. Arne tells them to leave him in peace, and they row home to Barrøy in two boats.

# 8

Nelvy's death is the type of death that prevents the bereaved from resuming their lives, those of them who thought they *had* a life, it is a profound and personal death, unlike anything they have to compare it with. So they rise from their beds late and walk around and do nothing. Their eating habits are irregular too, as Barbro is also stricken, they eat titbits and leftovers as the mood takes them, and have once again lost hope of both spring and peace materialising.

It is at this time that Ingrid discovers sleep, her body lying with renewed life between the sheets, as she dreams of something bearable, as she sees shimmering images and memories and an amusing incident, at which she is even able to smile, in her sleep, that is. Then she wakes and is just as insane and sits on the chamber pot and goes back to bed, to the same bearable dreams, such that an affection can arise between sleep and death.

When Barbro is on the mend and asks whether they are prepared to let themselves go to wrack and ruin out here, Ingrid turns her back on her in scorn and carries on sleeping and will not be moved, until Sverre bursts into her room one morning, red-faced and excited, and announces that the ewe has had three lambs, all of which have survived, and not one of them is a male.

From behind closed eyelids Ingrid says he is a good boy, but tells him to leave because she wants to get up and she is naked. His face can't get any redder and he stays put. Ingrid gets out of bed, slowly dresses and goes down to the cowshed with Sverre at her heels, unlike his brothers he is talkative and full of energy and cheerful, as if born to shine on both his elder and younger brother, and interpret for them, in some greater scheme; he doesn't resemble them in appearance, either, his hair is blond while theirs is dark.

Ingrid inspects the lambs and discusses the sheep's teats and milk with Barbro, then walks to the south of the island with her ears ringing beneath a sun which has no warmth, and here she sees that there are nests in the three Nelvy eider houses, as in all the others, this is going to be a bountiful spring.

She walks back and asks Barbro if they have ever had nests in all the houses. Barbro can't remember and makes no attempt to try; Ingrid says at any rate *she* can't.

Ingrid is eating a little more than she did before and tells Sverre not to go fishing with his brothers and to row her to Stangholmen. Arne says they haven't been out for over a week. Ingrid says it is high time they got cracking then. Sverre's face lights up. However, Ingrid doesn't sit next to him on the thwart, but in the stern with her hands on her belly and she still has a ringing in her ears and is blind to the sunshine and the smooth, glittering sea which they have waited for so long that they have forgotten what they are like.

She asks if Sverre wants to go back to Finnmark, too?

He is twelve years old and he says yes.

On Stangholmen she buys Thomas and Inga's two remaining sheep, as well as the four lambs they have just given birth to, together with two rolls of wire for the racks and their plough, which is almost new. She tells them they should spend all their money at once. Thomas says he knows, he has seen the scale of Margot's stockroom too; his son, Atle, will soon be coming to fetch them, so they can spend the rest of their lives somewhere on the mainland Ingrid has never heard of, so it is good that he has the opportunity to shake her hand before they leave.

Ingrid shakes Inga's hand, too.

Sverre rows back home while Ingrid, her ears still ringing, wonders whether to strip off all her clothes and stand up in the boat in the middle of the gleaming sea, it is a sledgehammer of an idea, for, as she waves goodbye to the elderly couple for the last time, she realises that her Russian is also dead, Alexander, the young engineer from Leningrad, he has been killed, and she will never see him again.

One ewe is startled by her cry and is about to jump into the sea, but Ingrid grabs it by the forelock and holds its head in her arms and does not shrink from mumbling words she is ashamed of. Sverre turns a deaf ear and carries on rowing. Safely home, Ingrid wonders how she has been able to get through yet another day.

When the brothers return, she examines the catch, listens

to Arne, who needs four new nets, tells them they should ask Barbro to get them ready, she has plenty of nets, and asks them to row to Stangholmen when they have finished gutting the fish, to fetch the plough that she and Sverre had no room for. After that she goes back to the house, and lies down, her ears still ringing, and dreams about things that are bearable, all manner of things, and about a perplexed smile on a face she thinks she recognises, but it is not always the same face, it fades and reappears, and her sleep is no longer a refuge.

Nevertheless, she doesn't get up.

She wastes away in bed, unable to sleep, until one morning a figure she doesn't recognise is sitting on the edge of her bed, it is Suzanne, and the sun's rays on the window bars in the north-east are so golden it must be evening, unless it is the morning and she is at the wrong end of the house, she sits up and looks around.

Suzanne is young and strikingly beautiful, although it is hard to put your finger on what it is that constitutes her beauty, or say anything meaningful about why she catches the eye, she just always has done. Now she looks tired and worried, has unnatural hemp-coloured curls in her shiny hair, lipstick on her lips and on one of her front teeth, which is slightly protruding, and she is wearing a white dress with embroidered yellow flowers and small, green sprigs of conifer, Ingrid smiles at her.

"Is it tha?"

Yes, Suzanne has arrived. She says:

"Hitler's dead."

And there is another stranger in the room, a boy of seven, maybe eight, in a smart travelling outfit and polished shoes, like a confirmand, he has fair, nicely combed hair and the same worried expression as his mother. "This is Fredrik," Suzanne says, Ingrid smiles at Fredrik and says:

"Hvur ar' tha, my bitty man?"

Fredrik looks at his mother in puzzlement, but Suzanne can't be bothered to translate. Ingrid hears the sound of hammering in the distance, squints in the direction of the window and asks what the noise is.

"Th' lads ar' builden' a hous'," Suzanne says, looking round the room where she grew up, in the years Ingrid tried her hand at being a mother and Suzanne at being a daughter.

"Has th' builden' material come?" Ingrid says.

"It must've done. They're busy at work at any rate, in Karvika of all places."

Suzanne rolls her eyes, and Ingrid gets up. Now she isn't naked, as she was when Sverre woke her and she had no option. She throws a dress over her shift and looks quite a lot paler than Suzanne as they go down to the kitchen where Barbro once again is in full command. Barbro's face lights up and she tells Ingrid that Suzanne keeps giving her hugs and pinching her plump stomach, there she goes again.

Ingrid doesn't get any hugs.

Suzanne has worked in a telephone exchange and can mimic dialects and speech defects and voices, and says:

"It is entirely understandable that Ingrid has had to take

to her bed, the situation here being as grave as it is."

She uses words like "captivating", "gosh" and "baguette", but can also – depending on the company she is in – switch to everyday speech, and Barbro serves coffee in cups made of Polish porcelain, which Suzanne recognises with a gasp and holds up to the light, as another worried furrow traverses her pretty brow and she mumbles something they don't understand.

Ingrid says they got the dinner set from her mother, Zezenie, around the time when Suzanne arrived on the island with her brother Felix. But their guest has no memory of this and puts down the cup again, stands up and says she has brought some presents for them, and she opens a trunk Ingrid hasn't noticed. Four kilos of coffee, an instrument she calls a spatula, and two irons are put on the table, one of them electric, as far as she can remember there aren't any irons on Barrøy, this place where there are only womenfolk, ha ha.

Ingrid says they don't even have electricity on the main island, but the flex is very nice, it looks like the line on a spanker sail. Suzanne says they can cut it off with pincers and use it as an old-fashioned flatiron – then thar'd bi one apiece, f'r Barbro an' Ingrid. But the spatula goes down best, after Suzanne has demonstrated how it works.

But in the midst of all this welcome jollity she raises a hand to her face, a hand with red nail varnish on all five fingers, and tells Ingrid she would like to see the island in the fine weather, she has been so looking forward to this, Fredrik can stay with his aunt, Barbro, can't he?

Ingrid and Barbro exchange glances, the boy is eating cinnamon biscuits spread with butter, which these fine townsfolk have brought with them, and the two younger women get no further than the yard before Suzanne bursts into a violent fit of sobbing;

"How horrid it is here!"

Ingrid stares, too stunned to speak.

"Hvur grim," she wails from the heart. "A can't mind it bein' *s'* grim . . ."

Ingrid has never viewed the island as more magnificent than now, this comes as a shock, either due to Suzanne's unexpected words or some sudden inner turmoil they set in motion. She turns her back on Suzanne and her nail varnish and strides over the hill to Karvika and watches as Arne and Helmer and Sverre lay the last sill timber on the foundations. They are all dressed in overalls, her father's and cousin's, partly taken in and partly taken up, and they have re-used the original holes in the rocks in the foundations, which they first took completely apart and then reconstructed, so everything is plumb and solid, but they are using new bolts, and Arne looks askance at Ingrid as she approaches, as do his brothers. Ingrid sees that the grass around the new buildings has been trampled flat and there are paths and tracks, the plot has been tamed and consecrated by man, it already looks inhabited, then she bends down and places both hands around the sill and pulls as hard as she can, and it doesn't budge.

# 9

And Barrøy is not horrid for long, Suzanne wakes up after one night's sleep in the South Chamber as her normal self, while Fredrik sleeps in Ingrid's old childhood room, in the bed where someone died not so long ago, but no-one says a word about that.

It turns out that in her trunk Suzanne also has some clothes more suited to Barrøy and the sea and to that concerned expression of hers, for which there so far has been no explanation. She is a living being among the dead, two people in one, an elegant, urbane, well-spoken lady who says "quite simply" one moment, and the next a woman who is able to inspect the building works in Karvika using all the local terminology; she can gut fish and repair nets and shear sheep, which they should have done a long time ago; now they are stuffing the wool into sacks and idly gossiping in muted voices about how much or how little they can get for it, not to mention in which type of currency or whether they might just as well hang on to it.

Suzanne thinks it is worth a lot as she sits and smells her

fingers and has to look up and shed a tear, which the others ignore. They also smile quietly to themselves when she squabbles with her cack-handed son, town boy Fredrik, who is no good at anything and has to have explained to him what a fish is, and a boat, a sea and an eider duck, subjects which even then don't interest him in the slightest. He keeps asking if they can do things the others have never heard of, and shudders, shamelessly, theatrically, when his mother tells him he has to gut the day's catch, which is just being landed by the Skarsvåg brothers, she scolds them for not having done it at sea. Grinning broadly, they ignore her.

They throw the catch into the basket and winch it up onto the quay, it is no small catch, and they climb up the ladder and stand admiring Fredrik's pathetic attempts with a knife, helped on his way by his mother's exasperated instructions. Ingrid tells her that he is as useless as Suzanne's brother was when they arrived here, our Felix, but tha can't mind it, eh?

No, Suzanne can't.

"No, hvur could tha?" Ingrid laughs. "Tha was three an' tha couldn't e'en walk."

"I can't remember that, either," Suzannne says, poking a finger in Helmer's chest and telling him that from now on it is his job to train her son.

Helmer glances up at Arne. Arne nods. Helmer grabs the knife and a cod weighing a good three kilos, thrusts his left index finger into the eye, forces his thumb under the jawbone and pushes the chalk-white belly upwards, shows Fredrik that it has been bled, here, so the blood can run out, that has to be done at sea, not the gutting though, then he sticks the point of the knife in about an inch down from the throat and slides it down to the anus so the guts tumble out and hang from a thin thread, slices the ear-bone and breaks the neck on the edge of the gutting bench, makes a couple more incisions and rips off the head, throws it aside and holds the end result in the air like a flag, sticks two fingers in the top of the cut and tugs out the remaining entrails in one go, asks Ingrid if she wants the liver, she says no, it's red, it's spring, and Helmer explains to Fredrik that those fish that are to be dried, like this one, shouldn't be slit open right up to the throat, places it beside one of a similar size on the bench, already gutted, sticks a hand down into the pile of twine and ties one length around the two tails, quickly winds it three times and holds the pair of fish aloft, while Ingrid says they should have finished the drying ages ago, it is too warm now, but they can't do any splitting either.

"Tha's forgot t' rinse 'em," Suzanne says.

Helmer blushes, chucks the two fish in the rinsing tub, drags them through the red water a few times and holds them up again to universal laughter. Even Fredrik laughs, and looks enquiringly up at his mother, who says:

"Now it's your turn. An' teach 'im hvur t' cut out th' tong', too. We're haven' fried tong' t'day."

But none of them knows how.

For the first time since the winter Ingrid goes into the new quay house and looks up at the white sky through the shattered slate roof, registers that there are no marks on the stone floor other than clean, wet water, locates the box with the spike, takes it outside so that Suzanne can show the four young men how to cut out tongues.

Ingrid smiles, impressed.

"She's deft at cutten'."

They take it in turns to try, put the cod head onto the spike, force open the mouth and copy the circular knife-cut that Suzanne showed them, leaving the tongues piled up on the spike. Each of them succeeds in his own way, even Fredrik, who receives a little extra tuition from his mother because he isn't that keen to stick his fingers in the cod-eyes, with the result that the heads slip out of his grasp, but he also receives more praise than he deserves because he goes for precision rather than speed, and has no interest in trying for both like the Finnmark boys.

Ingrid watches them until they are finished and have to hang the cod on the rack. She has walked around the outside of the quay house as if it were an unexploded bomb, now she has been inside, she has looked around and hasn't smelled anything but fish and sea and tar, and rotting seaweed, a smell of decay that belongs here, and her eyes have been blank and white and indifferent the whole time.

She asks Arne if he will repair the roof, they have enough slates, a roof ladder too, over there in the grass, not where it should be actually, it must have blown off the pegs holding it in place, and as she lifts the crate of tongues Barbro shouts up in the direction of the drying rack:

"Hang 'em on th' snag-stake, too!"

Which Fredrik has to have translated. Ingrid walks home with her aunt's voice ringing in her ears: "Teik 'em wi' th' crotch-rod!"

Which doesn't help much, there are snorts of laughter at any rate, and Ingrid is so strong after the fruitful visit to the quay house that she can reflect on those things about Nelvy that won't leave her, no-one has lived and died like Nelvy. And it occurs to her, as she starts on dinner in the kitchen at the end of this almost bearable day – potatoes and fried cod tongues – that she didn't know much about Nelvy's life, only about her death, and for that very reason she will never disappear, but return in the form of shock and boundless remorse and something even more important, which has to do with Ingrid's own inner darkness. But here in the kitchen she is alone and unseen, even Barbro is outside, she can hear her aunt's voice through the window she has opened to let the smoke out and the spring weather in, turns the tongues in white flour and fries them in margarine before laying them half on top of each other on a dish to form a perfect spiral, by then the potatoes are done, too.

# 10

Barrøy is a land of silence, the adults don't explain to their children what to do, they show them, and the children copy, and the inhabitants of Finnmark are like the Barrøyers, folk of few words and great wisdom in both hands and feet, whereas Fredrik asks *why* he has to hit a chisel with a hammer, questions that don't need answers, these things are just done – like this, almost nothing is done by means of words.

It is rumoured that Fredrik has taken piano lessons, which is yet another sign of his inability to adapt, but Barbro says the piano is fine, she listened to the piano when she was in hospital, and in church they have an organ, with keys, and the fact that this is an instrument that is operated using the hands contributes to Fredrik getting off more lightly than he deserves. But the very next day he storms into the kitchen, soaking wet, and hauls himself up onto his mother's lap.

"Goodness gracious," Suzanne says.

"He hit me," her son bawls.

"Who is *he*?"

"Him!"

He gesticulates wildly in the direction of the Finnmark boys, who have come in after him and lined up like a row of suspects, it was Helmer who hit him, the young man responsible for his training, but all the brothers were guilty of throwing him in the water, we had absolutely no choice, Arne mumbles.

Suzanne is about to fly at them, but Ingrid intervenes and asks why they did it.

Not even Fredrik wants to say why, and his eye is getting no less swollen with all that crying, it is beginning to turn black. However, Suzanne doesn't let up and it comes to light after a good deal of persuasion that Fredrik has thrown his tools in the sea because he is lazy and can't be bothered to work.

Fredrik screams that he *dropped* them by accident, the hammer and the two bolts, or was it three? And the Finnmark lads maintain their silence, standing like three soldiers before a military tribunal, until Suzanne looks down at her son, who by now has managed to get his sobbing under control and glances nervously up at his mother, waiting for the verdict. She says:

"But you can swim."

Barbro, bent over the washing-up bowl, chuckles, the others keep a straight face.

"But I can't *dive*!"

"Oh yes, you can!"

"It's cold!"

"What nonsense. If you've thrown the tools into the sea, you'll have to go and find them. Come here."

She drags him outside. The others follow them over the hill and down to Karvika, including Barbro, still chuckling. Helmer points down at the sea beyond the jutting rock which will form one of the moles sheltering the new quay. Fredrik looks up at his mother imploringly. But the sun is shining and there is no mercy. He edges his way down through the belt of seaweed, but has got no more than his ankles under water before he wails that it's cold, cold . . .

Arne takes some deep breaths and looks at Ingrid. She nods. He kicks off his boots and strips down to the waist, brushes Fredrik aside, dives in and is gone for a long time.

They see him below the green water, like a flapping, white bird, until he disappears completely. Then he emerges again, with the hammer but without the bolts, scrambles up onto the barnacled rock and he cannot speak, his lips are blue, as he stands amid the tangled seaweed shivering, and is all muscle and sinew, a perfect da Vinci anatomical drawing, like the one that hangs in every single schoolroom along the coast. Ingrid has brought along a blanket and drapes it over him, telling him to take off his pants and his brothers to pummel him.

It turns into a game and a brawl, with them all trading punches, until Arne gets back his voice and can tell them to go to hell. They watch as he dries his body, naked beneath the blanket. Then they follow him up the hill again, like in a procession, along the path the boys have trodden in Karvika, where others very rarely go, even now, it is hard for them to get used to the idea, but they are changing, beginning to accept the idea that one day some good can come even of a curse, and none of them fails to hear Suzanne calling her son an idiot.

Ingrid stops and looks at her. Suzanne looks down and says:

I know, I know.

She carries on walking, with the boy in tow. Everyone also hears the next thing she says: "Cretin."

But they don't know what it means.

That same evening Arne comes to see Ingrid, who is tending the lambs in the southernmost garden, and he says there is a boat on the seabed in Karvika.

She looks at him. Then she asks him why he is telling her this now, and when they are alone. He shrugs.

"Tha's got kien eyes," she says.

Arne says yes, there is nothing wrong with what is left of his eyesight, he found the hammer, but not the bolts. Ingrid says that doesn't matter, he should sit in the grass while she remains standing, in case somebody sees them from the houses.

He does as she says.

She tells him what type of boat it is, where it came from and what it was carrying, and she can tell him everything without her eyes flickering, as in happy moments at the hospital, or when she told Barbro, and the only important thing she omits is the love, which is not her word anyway but the doctor's, and she ends up saying that Arne shouldn't tell anyone else, it has nothing to do with them.

He nods and looks as though he knows she is holding something back, but that he is still content to be initiated into half a secret. But then his eye tells her he is wondering whether the time is ripe to ask her whether she has ever been married, or has a husband, her belly is large now, as if that had anything to do with the boat at the bottom of the sea in Karvika, so Ingrid turns and walks up towards the houses.

## 11

Something happened to the island as Arne rose like a faun out of the ice-cold sea, a ticking in a much vaster clock than the one which is still confused on the wall in the house: the last snow falls, lands on green shoots and is gone in minutes, tarred boats lie with their bellies in the air and have to be shielded from the sun by tarpaulins, spring is no longer evasive and furtive, it grabs them by the scruff of the neck, it is upon them, like a summer.

The main structure of one wall is finished, the potato field has been tilled with the new plough, drawn by Arne and Barbro, while the others sow the seed for the autumn harvest, bent backs over steaming, brown soil, and there is food and coffee outdoors.

Fredrik does his best, which still isn't good enough, Ingrid looks after the eider ducks and sheep, casts a worried eye over the stockfish for worms and Armageddon, and Suzanne isn't averse to flirting with Arne; she asks him why he has only one eye, is it so he can see her better, in her new dress, and shouldn't she cut his long hair, he looks like a girl.

Ingrid, who is more restrained, has to walk away, but only as far as her vantage point on the hill overlooking the bay so that she can follow the conversation, Arne on the ladder propped against another wall, Suzanne on the ground, shouting up to him in the sunshine, and for the first time Ingrid sees a smile on the face of the eldest Skarsvåg brother, who says he will be seventeen next week; he has finally told her when their birthdays are, Ingrid considers these dates important, everyone is entitled to a birthday, she has marked them on her calendar. Suzanne has just turned twenty-two, and Fredrik will soon be seven, but according to his mother he can already read.

As they stand there in their own splendid ways in the spring weather a blast rings out in the air, a foghorn from the Fourth Book of Moses, a black and white mountain detaches itself from the mainland and floats slowly across the placid, glistening fjord, it seems to be coming from the trading post, but it is the coastal steamer, which in both normal and abnormal times plies its route on the inland side of the main island, a steamer off course, and it is bearing the Norwegian flag, not only on its masts and funnels, bow and stern, it is fluttering from every single rope, cable and chain like a Christmas tree decoration, and the horn keeps blaring, sheep and birds are silenced and stand with the island folk on the rocks staring out at this monster of a ship gliding closer to Barrøy than anything of this size has ever ventured. People are crammed side by side along the rails waving hats and caps and elbows and knees as though they are making fun of the islanders, the boat radiates jubilation and the dawn of a new era, it is a floating festive horde of revellers who have left their senses, it is May 10.

The Barrøyers stand rigid, speechless, and are aware that the sight when it eventually disappears will leave them with an immense sense of loss, even though they don't understand what they have seen and they wave back only when the ship has passed, and continue to do so until they feel stupid. But there can be no doubt that they have witnessed a revelation, something that lifts the mood of a whole island and stirs them into life. Ingrid runs off for the telescope that has already deceived so many eyes and she watches as the immense ship merges into the horizon and becomes a black dot beneath a pale moon.

As a result Barrøy is no longer mute and withdrawn, the people there are all talking at once about something they haven't understood, and Barbro yells that they should slachter a bloody lamb an' have meat t' eat.

They cheer before Ingrid has a chance to collect her thoughts, so she agrees, and the lamb is slaughtered, carved up and cooked, and they continue to talk all at once over the meal in the parlour, as if both the winter and the war were over, and discuss all the opportunities and changes that may bring, in heaven and on earth.

But as they sit gorged, waiting for Suzanne to serve what she calls a compôte and the others call soup, it is a soup too, it is red, with sago and raisins, Ingrid's eyes wander along the walls and stop at a painting of a sailing ship her father once staggered home with, and she bursts into tears, no sobs or any other sounds, only a stream of still water. No-one understands, not even she does, and Arne says that now Ingrid is thinking about Nelvy again.

Suzanne puts the tureen on the table, asks who Nelvy is and no-one answers.

She asks again and dishes out the soup and distributes bowls around the table. Ingrid gets up and places a hand on Arne's shoulder, as though he were her son, then walks outside into a shower of rain and sits down in Bosom Acre with the first sheep, which she has christened Lea, after a woman in the Bible who lived in the shadow of her sister, but who was blessed with many more offspring than her, she sits with her face buried in wet fleece, until she walks away and dries her face and is able to join the others, who are still discussing the significance of the ship, their laughter isn't even strained.

However, Ingrid's mind is still on what Arne said about her thinking about Nelvy, because she had been, but most of all she had been thinking about the engineer from Leningrad, and suddenly she had the feeling that he must still be alive, this is what has shaken her to the core, along with the life inside her, she can feel the kicking, and from now on she won't shed a single tear.

# 12

Reluctantly, Ingrid allows herself to be rowed over to the trading post by Arne. She sits on the aft thwart with a blanket over her shoulders, holding her belly. And this is a strange experience, as the Barrøyers never row anywhere without an objective, and neither those remaining nor the young man rowing knows the purpose of this trip. And they have Fredrik with them, as Arne won't allow him to be alone with his brothers, he doesn't get seasick, but he won't row.

At the trading post they hear that the war really is over, and sure enough they are going to introduce a new currency, the world is rising from the ashes once again. The foreman is also new, a young man from the mainland with energetic, bristly hair, and eyes that are far too large, unless his face is too small, he says they should just bring along whatever they have in the way of eggs, fish, down, it is more important than ever now to keep the wheels turning.

And the prices?

There are some things that never change.

The Germans have left in a hurry and the liberators, the British, have dumped their cannons and military hardware in the sea so that the Norwegians can buy new artillery in Britain as soon as they get back on their feet. Incidentally, the British are nowhere to be seen, either, but the Norwegians are. Men, women, and children have streamed out of their houses, looking newly scrubbed and white in the sunshine. An auction is being held in the former camp, on offer is whatever has been left behind by the Germans, stinking wardrobes and battered office furniture with drawers full of mothballs, pen nibs and rubber stamps bearing the Third Reich eagle, standard lamps and armchairs and items of clothing that are of no use to anyone. The rubber wheels from the gun carriages at the Fort are also of interest, they can be cut into suitable sizes and used as shoe soles. And not least the horses, the same horses that the Germans commandeered when they arrived, now five years older and ground down by the horrors of war as they stand scowling in their halters. But they are recognised by their old masters, and, it transpires, even have Norwegian names, which slowly wake them from their torpor amid the shouting and the bidding, which is done for reasons of both necessity and sentimentality.

Ingrid is wearing a dress she was given by Suzanne, which doesn't make her look strange, in her own or others' eyes, and she, too, wonders whether she should buy a horse, with the money she doesn't have, but is distracted by the collective hubbub: there is a peaceful carnival atmosphere, all the faces she sees again, wearing cautious, fresh and expectant expressions. Anja has moved out of the rectory with her four children, along with Gunvor, and moved into the spacious house of a fishing skipper in the village, a man Ingrid knows from her schooldays, who never managed to get married, but looks as though he might well succeed in doing so now, he has a wide-brimmed hat on his head, is holding Ante's hand and has handed out rock sugar in brown paper bags to the whole bunch. Anja whispers to Ingrid that her husband probably won't recover, she has it in writing, look.

Ingrid has a letter thrust into her hand and recognises the handwriting of Erik Falc, the doctor, and remembers something she immediately forgets, as the children are no longer shy, they take her hand and look well dressed and well fed, peace children, full of mischief, and as she is about to ask Gunvor something to do with Nelvy – Arne is looking straight at her, as always, it is as if he has become her guard, while Fredrik is unable to take his eyes off the horses – Ingrid comes to a decision that has troubled her ever since she was overcome by those strange feelings in connection with the engineer's life and death.

She leaves all the hustle and bustle behind and strides up the white road above the rectory, the two youths at her heels, before turning into a red house belonging to the person who was once the village chieftain, a large, towering man.

Nobody answers when she knocks, but a rankling far back in her memory causes her to open the door and go in, and she sees that the house is a mess, a house without a woman, with a man sprawled over the kitchen table amid dirty plates and cups, in a place which presumably once was very presentable, he looks as if he wants to be buried, and mumbles just as despairingly as when she arrived on the *Salthammer* last winter:

"It's you, is it?"

His debilitated state puts her sufficiently at ease to sit down, while Arne and Fredrik stay on their feet, looking for something to rest their eyes on. She asks Henriksen if he still has the papers from his time as chairman of the Rations and Relocation Board.

No, he snaps, and continues to eye her until he realises all hope is gone, makes a half-hearted attempt to get to his feet then motions towards a chest of drawers buried beneath a pile of clothes and overalls. Ingrid gets up and pushes the clothes aside, pulls out one drawer, hears an irritable no, opens the next and sees a card-index file with five columns, a last vestige of order.

He says she will have to search, damned if he is going to do it.

She flicks through the alphabet and finds something that looks like a postcard without a stamp, with the name Jadviga from Mehamn written on it in a shaky hand. No surname, date or place of birth, earlier place of abode, or age, only that she was an evacuee staying with the Abelsen family in Finnvika, together with two boys Ingrid remembers from the galley on the *Salthammer*, and also the captain who buried Nelvy, Lukas Wara; they are all on the same card, only the boys' dates of birth are given, they are in their mid-teens, and they aren't brothers.

Ingrid knows that Abelsen lives on the southern tip of the main island, but enquires nonetheless, and for the last time hears this voice that has lost all authority. Henriksen says how the hell should I know, and Ingrid, who has wished death and agony on him for the past six months, decides that he is already dead, or at least in such a bad way that he is beginning to arouse her sympathy, so she sticks the card down her dress and hurries out.

He calls after them, saying he has saved her life, she has to testify for him . . .

Ingrid walks back down to the village, past the auction and into the store, where Margot is nowhere to be seen, but one of her assistants tells her that Motor Markus, which has become her son's name in the course of the past year, has been sent away, they say for good, so if Ingrid wants a lift she will have to go with the dairy van, which in truth is more like a tractor, and Ingrid still doesn't tell Arne what she is up to, nor does he enquire, and Fredrik doesn't care, he asks if they can have some sweets, there are some gumdrops and chocolate buttons in the glass jars over there on the counter.

Ingrid says no.

Then she pauses and asks whether he has ever eaten chocolate.

He says, yes, lots of times.

She asks when.

He seems to be looking for an answer that will appease her, and Ingrid lets the matter drop.

*

Jakob Abelsen in Finnvika is old, he is a widower, has fished from rowing boats with both Ingrid's father and grandfather and remembers them and the fishing banks so well that he can't stop himself rambling on about them as soon as he sees her. With him on the well-run farm – which has as many as six farmhands – lives a middle-aged maid, who seems to have plans to become the woman of the house, unless she already is so. The two young boys from the galley on the *Salthammer* are planting potatoes in a newly ploughed field and Jadviga is reclining in a rocking chair in the sunlight streaming through a large parlour window. She is sleeping peacefully with her mouth open, and wakes as the maid places a hand on her knee and tells her they have visitors, she asks if they would like some coffee?

Ingrid says yes.

It takes time for Jadviga to come round, and the coffee is on the table before Ingrid can find the sheet of paper and place it in Jadviga's lap, the page from the sketch pad with three identical verses in one single column. Jadviga holds it at a good distance from her eyes, squints and smiles, her whole face a mass of white wrinkles.

"It says I love you."

She runs a thick, deformed nail down over the lines and says: "Nine times."

"The same?" Ingrid asks. "*Nine times?*"

Jadviga counts the lines again and says yes, nine times, takes her cup, examines it and moves it slowly to her lips.

Ingrid asks:

"Nothing else, no name, address . . . ?"

"No."

The window has just been cleaned and is crystal clear, she can see for miles, a white sheet falls across her field of vision, the meadows are green and sway in the summer breeze, beyond them the same sea stretches into the distance as he writes the identical lines nine times without telling her what she really wants to know, and what is more with a wry smile on his face.

Another sheet falls across her vision, and her fingers tremble as she folds the paper and waves it at the window, as if someone is out there. Jadviga drinks her coffee and calmly watches her.

Ingrid places her hand on Jadviga's knee and says thank you, goes out into the summer warmth and feels a need to walk around the house, past a grindstone, a stack of wood and a peat shed, a spade left in the ground, the shaft broken. In the farmyard she sees not only Arne and Fredrik and the two young boys, laughing at something, but also old Abelsen, pipe in mouth, listening to the captain, Lukas Wara, who is in the middle of a long discourse about wanting to go home.

Ingrid hurries over and says that the authorities – the new ones, too – have banned them from returning, she has seen the notice in the store. Wara snorts and says he doesn't give a shit, he's off home, even if it means going on foot, it can't be more than a couple of thousand kilometres.

The others laugh. But the captain has at last received a letter he can rely on, telling him that as much as a third of his town has survived, including his small barn, he can sleep there until he has rebuilt the farmhouse, it is summer, it is light all day and night.

Jakob chuckles, and takes the pipe out of his mouth.

"Come on, it'd be better for you to stay here. You're too old."

"It's like being in the workhouse here!"

"What? Is there something wrong with the grub?"

"What are you two blathering on about?" shouts the maid, who has come out onto the front steps.

"He's not happy with the food," Jakob shouts.

She shouts something back, which they don't hear, then goes inside, slamming the door behind her. Jakob's smile vanishes and he says, you don't have anyone to go back to.

Wara looks as though he is about to implode, but repeats that it is humiliating to be wasting his time here on another man's land when he has his own.

"Oh, go to hell then," Jakob says, and turns to the boys. "Haven't you got any potatoes to plant?"

Ingrid says they will have to be getting on their way. Jakob takes them part of the way by tractor, still rambling on about the sea and the years in Lofoten, memories she has no space for. Nor can she bring herself to ask about the ship going down, as if she can't accommodate that, either, and on the trailer, Fredrik too finds his tongue, as if peace has also had an impact on him, he wants to know where Finnmark is, and Skarsvåg.

Arne tells him and Fredrik asks about the war in the north. Well, there are only ashes left, and Fredrik is eager to know more, while Arne becomes wearier and wearier with every answer he utters. As they walk down to the trading post, they haven't even bought any provisions, Ingrid forgot, so they go back up and buy what they need, on tick, and as they walk down to the trading post for a second time, Arne tells her they will soon have run out of building materials.

Ingrid was expecting him to say something else, and she answers that she knows.

Three walls, Arne adds, one of them with wood panels as well as the roof trusses, what's she going to do about it?

Ingrid repeats that she doesn't know, it depends on him.

He asks her what *she* thinks.

You boys are leaving, aren't you?

He says it is obvious what *he* wants, but *she* always seems to be the one making the decisions. To which Ingrid says nothing.

On the way home to Barrøy, Fredrik is still talking, now about his own father, whom neither he nor Suzanne has mentioned before; he is clearly still alive and works for a business selling something Fredrik cannot elaborate on, but it transpires that he is seldom or never around.

Arne asks why.

Fredrik says his father is busy. Arne says:

"Doing what?"

Fredrik says it is something important. Arne doesn't get any further with that, either, and Fredrik starts defending his absent father, who he gathers has fallen into disfavour, until a step-father turns up, he is German and called Armin, he doesn't see much of him, either.

"Armin?" Arne says.

Sitting on the thwart, Fredrik squirms, and can find no port of refuge, even though Ingrid says she is sure Armin is a nice man.

Fredrik stares imploringly at Arne, who casts himself over the oars, rows on at a back-breaking speed and asks, isn't it about time the pianist learned to row.

What do you mean, Fredrik already *can*.

He sits at Arne's side and they row in zigzag fashion without exchanging a word, through the drizzle that is beginning to fall on the choppy sea, while Ingrid keeps an eye on what is going on between them, counts her money and explores her memories to escape something that is beginning to overwhelm her.

When they have put the boat away, Arne says to Fredrik, oh, well, that's another day you've survived, then puts the provisions in a fish crate, hoists it onto his shoulder and walks towards the house.

Ingrid takes Fredrik's hand and says everything will turn out fine for him on Barrøy, but he shouldn't think anymore about these fathers of his, nor talk about them. Fredrik says, yes, it's a nice island. Ingrid says loudly that peace is not much different from war, and goes straight up to the North Chamber and takes out the sheet of paper with the nine lines from beneath her dress, because she wants to burn it.

But how can she do that in the North Chamber, there is no stove.

She is in the North Chamber because she needs to be alone

as she re-reads the lines, and she doesn't go down again that day. Instead she lies beneath the eiderdown, and once more she knows he is dead, she can sense it in her body, a dual paralysis, of greater and lesser magnitude, a steel string that vibrates through her whole existence.

But then she gets up again, goes to the window and looks north across the fields and the sea towards Oterholmen, and suddenly she feels she must be alive after all, either dead or alive, she *can't* die, all according to where she is in this room, where she paces back and forth all evening, and which she now knows she will never be able to leave, no matter how hard the frost may be in the winter. Suzanne will have to stay in the South Chamber.

# 13

With peace comes the return of Johannes Malmberget, the priest. No-one knows where he has been, but he is such an integral part of the islands that no-one asks, he is so ancient that, of his old self, only his voice is left.

It booms out, however, after his two youngest sons have carried him to the altar and sat him in an armchair with a microphone and a discarded German loudspeaker. The locals think it sounds like a speech from London on a banned radio and are on the point of applauding. And again he focuses on the question that has puzzled him all his life and has been a faithful component of every single sermon he has written: is man great or small?

For the first time they also understand what his position on this matter is, for he has come to a conclusion: man is great.

For a moment they wonder whether the war has reduced the priest to banalities, but he justifies his answer using stirring words such as staunch and steadfast, mightiest mountains and the tiniest grain of sand, that which shall never perish, at the end he also manages to find a place for Jesus' resurrection and ascension to heaven, although it is neither Easter nor Whitsun but the first Sunday after the Feast Day of St John the Baptist; his tired clichés about salt and the skerries and the islands are fresh and sparkling again, as if hewn from stone.

In a grandiloquent finale he bellows: many of you are no doubt familiar with developments around the world; seen in that perspective we up here on the grey margins are fortunate, as absurd as that may seem; this may not be obvious, but please dwell on it for a while and see if you don't recognise the truth in the words of a wise man, not mine, the Lord's.

A murmur runs through the uplifted congregation, attendance is good, almost every single survivor has returned. Ingrid sees Nelly again, she has spent the winter in Havstein, and her family, friends from her schooldays, Jenny and Hanna with the cats, and not least Anja, who has left the skipper, taking all her children, and has a ticket north on the coastal steamer, she isn't going home, but to a reception camp, to meet her husband who apparently has recovered after all. She looks a little sorry, but she is no longer in that war-ravaged, indefinable age between twenty and sixty, looking more like the twenty-nine-year-old registered in Henriksen's papers, and Ingrid says she won't forget them, they mustn't forget her, either, they have to write.

Anja asks how *she* is?

Ingrid looks at her and says she doesn't know, yet, and places a hand on Sara's head.

*

Ingrid has asked to have a word with the priest. His sons carry him down the nave, lower him into the sidecar of a German motorbike they bought at the auction and trundle him down between the graves so that the meeting can be as private as Ingrid wants it to be.

She confides to Johannes Malmberget that she is with child, as though he hadn't noticed, her clothes are loose and summery, and she doesn't want any stigmas attached to this child, the priest is the best person to guarantee this.

He does, too, with a mere flourish of the hand, likewise without even asking who the father is. To be on the safe side, she says he was a resistance fighter, and was hiding in the islands.

"Is he alive?" the priest asks.

Ingrid nods. And the priest is sceptical, there are so many children without a father here, this is not farming country, where the men are safely shut up behind closed doors with their wives and children all year round, Ingrid should be happy to have this gift, a new life, has she thought about what to call the child?

"Alexander."

The priest says that isn't a very common name here. Ingrid agrees.

"And if it's a girl?"

"Kaja."

"Ah, that was your grandmother's name."

He promises to stay alive until he has christened the child.

And then he has a matter of his own to discuss with her,

he sticks an unsteady hand inside his waistcoat and pulls out a wallet, which he hands to her. Ingrid steps back. He tells her in a loud voice to take it. But she isn't nineteen anymore and mentions the letter he sent her at the hospital, containing money, the infamous letter, the significance of which she recalls, and says that after all these years she finally wants a clarification of the strange relationship between him and her father, and the conversation comes to a halt.

Johannes Malmberget can't so easily call for help, so their eyes wander around the graves, known and unknown names on the headstones and crosses, the wild flowers and the lush meadows down to the sea, the grass is high already, and Ingrid's cheeks are red, but she repeats the request.

Without looking at her, he says in his previous life he borrowed some money from the village bank, the small, rundown savings bank, to help one of his numerous sons, who wasn't up to much, he has to admit, he is dead now, with Barrøy as a security, for which he paid her father a small amount, there was no liability on his part.

"No liability on the *loan*?"

"Well, no, in a way."

"A priest has his own property though, hasn't he?" Ingrid says.

Yes, he does, but . . . that was mortgaged as well, she got half of what he owed when she was at the hospital, and this is the rest, does she understand what he's telling her?

Ingrid says no, but she can accept the money as a loan.

"A loan?"

"Yes."

"But it's *your* money."

"Is it new money or old?"

He laughs mirthlessly and asks if she hopes he is going to die soon.

Ingrid asks whether that was what he had hoped about her father, and the priest looks both unhappy and angry, and mumbles that the money is at any rate good enough to spend in Margot's store, by the way her son is back now and is being hailed as a good patriot and resistance fighter.

Ingrid sticks the wallet inside her cardigan and is about to say that the priest came at the right moment, but realises that in fact he hasn't, he has come too late, now as before.

Johannes Malmberget casts an eye over the people who have gathered outside the church, in groups dressed in black, their voices muted next to the house of God and they will grow louder the further they get from it and turn into frivolous laughter as soon as they are far enough away. He raises an arm to summon his sons, but they can't see him. Ingrid has to shout, and they come trotting up as the old man says it was wonderful to hear Barbro today, what a voice.

"But she still doesn't know the words, does she," the priest says.

"No."

"No, no, of course not."

Ingrid hurries over to the others, who ask what she has been talking to the priest about. She isn't sure herself yet, something to do with the christening, she says.

But back on Barrøy that evening, she takes Barbro for a walk through the gardens to the south and tells her about the money, she has counted it now, it is exactly the same amount as she received at the hospital, she spent all that on building materials for Karvika, on sheep, food and a plough, and much besides, but she doesn't reveal the precise figure, instead she asks her aunt whether she thinks Suzanne has come to the island to hide.

The question takes Barbro by surprise.

Ingrid asks whether Fredrik has talked to her about his father – he is still tied to her apron strings after all – not to mention his stepfather or uncle.

Barbro says no and mutters that Suzanne hasn't said anything, either.

Ingrid says he is German.

Barbro asks who is German.

The stepfather.

Barbro is still confused.

"She war fourteen whe' she left," she says hazily.

"It's *peace* teim nu," Ingrid says in a loud voice.

"That's hva tha thinks," Barbro says petulantly and asks if that is supposed to mean they should put up that stupid light again, the lighthouse.

Ingrid rolls her eyes and says, to calm her down, that it is also time to write the letter.

What letter?

To Lars, we're going to be alone this winter, three women and one young boy who is starting school.

Barbro answers that the Finnmark lads are here, but the next moment she adopts a sheepish expression, which puts Ingrid on her guard.

She says perhaps we may be able to hold on to the Finnmark boys until past the haymaking season, if we're lucky, what is on Barbro's mind?

Barbro has to come out with it – the letter has already been written.

"*Hva?!*"

Yes, by Suzanne, under Barbro's supervision, she even dictated a few words herself, it has been sent too, not to Lars, but to Felix, they have fished together for years, and if anyone can persuade Lars to come south again, it is Felix, Arne sent it several weeks ago.

"*Arne* did *hva*?!"

Barbro turns, flings out both arms and yells above the wet clover and buttercups that she is bloody sick of Ingrid's whingeing, and her fists swing like oscillating clubs at her sides as she marches up to the house through the knee-high grass.

Ingrid waits until she has disappeared through the porch door, takes a deep breath and heads slowly towards the cliffs in the west, follows the sea-smoothed rocks north past the anchor bolt and nets that are no longer there and reaches the Swedes' quay house, where the Skarsvåg brothers have hammered an iron hook into a post and are teaching Fredrik how to attach sinker stones to line floats.

Ingrid feels as if she is intruding, Fredrik's chubby baby-face and the naïve expression that still doesn't belong here, Helmer and Sverre exercising self-restraint, the three of them each sitting on his own line tub, resting their elbows on their knees and fidgeting with their fingers as if they lack a prayer. Fredrik is standing with a sinker stone in his small hands trying to attach it to the line, he, too, looks up in surprise when she appears.

Ingrid takes Arne behind the quay house, puts two fingers in the breast pocket of his newly washed shirt and tugs, as if to pull him towards her, then pushes him away again and asks if they can stay on Barrøy until after the haymaking.

He looks at her with his one eye and stretches out his arm too, runs his fingertips along her upper arm, it is late in the afternoon and chilly and the dew glistens on their hair and skin, he says he doesn't know what his brothers want, they haven't talked about Finnmark for ages, they have started to forget, they are still young.

Ingrid asks him what *he* wants. She needs a clear answer now.

He withdraws his hand and says he doesn't know, either.

Yes, he does, she says.

Yes, he says.

She turns her back on him and takes a few steps, looks round and says he can come to her in the North Chamber tonight, but doesn't bother to find out whether he has understood. She calls to Fredrik, walks with him up to the house and tells Barbro it was good they wrote the letter to Felix, let's hope he can persuade Lars, goodness gracious, and slaps Suzanne round the face. What's that for, she asks, but looks as though she feels it might be deserved. Ingrid takes a pail of water with her and goes upstairs without eating and washes and lies down with the same trembling in her body as in the winter, the same freezing sensation, but not with the same warmth.

Arne sneaks barefoot up the stairs to her room, when the light is at its darkest and everyone is asleep. She tells him to be careful and stand behind her so that the baby won't be harmed. He is ardent and rough, and it doesn't take long. She says he can't sleep there, not in this room, but she hopes he and his brothers will stay until the season is over, until they have finished all the work on the islands. He says something, but she doesn't hear what, it sounds like sniffling, and she doesn't investigate. He puts his hands around her belly, they are hot and hard, like a cracked shell around a colossal egg. After he has gone, as noiselessly as he came, she misses his hands, but falls asleep in no time and does not dream.

# 14

There is no normal haymaking this summer, the earth has lain fallow for the two years that have passed since Barbro and Ingrid last did the mowing – and only very superficially at that, compared with the years before – when they were also alone and trying to maintain the tradition from the time the men were there, using hired labourers from Havstein who were not driven by the same dedication.

The mowing machine now stands idle and rusting between the stone walls, and the scythe keeps getting caught in the clumps of old grass, so they curse more than they mow, and have to cut the grass at mid-calf height. Ingrid can't bear to watch and goes so far as to sell eider down at a time of the year when down shouldn't be sold, it is a breach of tradition, but she can't touch the priest's money, for she doesn't fully understand its origins.

She sells not only the two kilos from this year's ducks, but also one of the old sacks in the barn. Then she goes to see the ever-willing Adolf, who ships over not one, but two horses. He doesn't come himself, he sends his son, Daniel, who uses the opportunity to tell the Barrøyers that their island is a sinking ship, what a sorry sight . . . He says – at the sight of the guillotined grass that sticks out on the hayracks like straw and blows off at the slightest gust of wind and has to be raked together and hung again – that they can't re-plough all the gardens, but he can bring over a kind of harrow and also a roller with spikes that can tear up the old stuff, they will have to pick out the worst clods by hand, as well as the stones, and deposit all this shite in a pile in the hollow over there, he says, and hope that one day a tree might grow from it, ha ha.

As soon as the haymaking is finished and the posts and wires have been cleared away, they start on this job, which has never been done on Barrøy before. And Daniel sees not only what is, but also what can be, he is a cheery, reckless and forward-looking man of twenty-five who works more or less round the clock for a hefty wage, which Ingrid has promised him in secret. But when he wants to bring in three youths he knows from Havstein Ingrid says it would be better if he brought over the two young refugees from Abelsen's in Finnvika, the man will be only too happy to be rid of them now his crops are harvested, she remembers her father's description of Jakob Abelsen, a good man, but greedy.

Daniel sails over to the main island and on his return says they won't come without Jadviga. Ingrid says all three of them can come. Daniel asks what they should do about the old captain, Lukas Wara. Ingrid laughs and says he has probably settled in at Jakob's, but he is also welcome to come, if he wants.

Daniel sails over again and returns with the two young men and Jadviga, whom they carry up to the house on a stretcher made of hayrack poles and lower into the rocking chair in the kitchen, where she looks around and says it is a nice house, is there any coffee?

Indeed, Lukas Wara has settled in at the Abelsens, now he has injured a foot, a circumstance which has not made him any less grumpy.

The two boys are called Benjamin and Jørgen, they are sixteen and seventeen, and say they can't stay long on Barrøy, for they have been told that their parents and siblings have been found and are in a camp outside Harstad waiting for the authorities to give them permission to return home, they will meet them in the camp.

Daniel tells them Ingrid will find someone to take them north and pay them for their work if they delay their departure by a month.

They give it some thought. Arne says:

"What about us?"

"You, too," Ingrid says, and adds – although she doesn't know – that *Barrøy II* will be arriving from Lofoten within the next few weeks, it can take them to the nearest port of call.

They look at each other, also at Daniel, and nod, but not one of them says an audible "yes".

Benjamin and Jørgen have brought along all sorts of clothes and some worn-out tools, which they were given by Jakob, and Jadviga fits into Barbro's old clothes and also old Martin's bed in the closet off the sitting room, she can go there under her own steam. She whiles away the days in the rocking chair in the kitchen with Barbro, whom she surprises, in between naps, with small, absurd memories of a world no-one has ever heard of, she also asks how many children Barbro has.

"One."

Jadviga has five. She holds up her hand and shows her five fingers. Barbro asks where they are.

Jadvika closes her eyes.

At the beginning of September three of the nine gardens not only look like newly ploughed fields, but also as though they have been created by love. They transport the sheep over to Gjesøya and get to grips with the next garden while Barbro bakes and cooks for the whole crew, and Ingrid hands over more and more of the responsibility to Daniel and Arne, and picks berries, makes jam and juice and calculates how many sheep she can afford to feed with the coming harvest, counts loads of hay and animals, including the cow they don't yet have, and concludes it may be enough, this *maybe*, which is a mantra in every fisherman-cum-farmer's deadly serious attitude to life.

As no boat has appeared on the horizon by the time the fourth garden has been finished, she accepts Daniel's suggestion that they start on a new plot, he likes it on Barrøy, which Ingrid suspects has something to do with Suzanne, she too works with ardour and a bent back in the fields alongside the boys, pulling up tufts and picking up stones without a whimper, and then they have to barrow out the muck from the cowshed, lots of that here, not much else, Daniel laughs.

Now Ingrid has wheedled out of Suzanne how things stand with her two husbands: the first was a Norwegian Nazi and the second – Armin – was a German non-commissioned officer who was shot by his own for stealing ration coupons and food for her and Fredrik, among others, from a depot he was in charge of, she wasn't married to either of them.

Ingrid asks if this is the whole truth.

Suzanne yawns and looks as if this is true enough for a lawless outpost like this.

Ingrid asks why she didn't say anything about Fredrik in her letters. Suzanne says she didn't think it was worth mentioning, his father didn't want anything to do with him. So Ingrid leaves it at that. No, she does ask one question, what name did Suzanne go under during these years, Tommesen or Barrøy.

"Tommesen," Suzanne says.

Ingrid says perhaps she should stop using this name and begin to use Barrøy, at any rate that is the name *she* used when she registered Fredrik at the school.

"The school, yes . . ."

Suzanne nods slowly.

Ingrid also says she should stay with Fredrik in Havstein for the first week of school, she can stay with Nelly, whom she may remember, Ingrid has already arranged this as well.

"Th' girl wi' a stammer?"

"Yes, she stammers."

But it wasn't this that was foremost in Suzanne's mind, this was just a passing thought, what she really wanted to know was why she had to be with Fredrik in Havstein.

Ingrid doesn't feel any inclination to answer that, because even though Fredrik has been almost half a man in the fields and stopped throwing tools into the sea ages ago, he is as he is.

So mother and son leave in the rowing boat one crystal-clear morning, the sun and an invisible haze making their eyes flicker and squint, they arrive only two weeks late, this too is an old Barrøyer tradition.

And it is while Suzanne and Fredrik are in Havstein that Ingrid is brought to her knees, the time has come, there has been no lack of counting and calculating the days, and it is on the early side, all depending on how you view it. She has no wish to let the others witness it either, so she carefully puts down her half-full berry bucket on the grass and staggers down to the boat shed and slides out the færing using the winch, scrambles on board and grasps the oars and tries to row, but gets no further than ten to twelve fathoms out before she falls to the boards in the prow, with her screams summoning the others.

The whole gang come running down, she can see them over the newly painted gunwale, they stand in a line between the boat shed and the high-water marker staring out at her and the boat, there have never been so many young people on Barrøy who don't belong there, seven of them. Ingrid can see their heads, their various heights and the colours and lengths of their hair, through a green mist, her breathing is like a piston pumping inside her. In their midst stands Barbro, mouth agape and an arm waving in the air helplessly, the sky is grey today and the sea as white as a snow-covered plain.

It is a difficult birth, brutal but short. Ingrid does as Barbro tells her and kneels between the thwarts. And once again it is Arne who strips down and swims out. He scrambles into the boat, but he can't bear to see human blood in the space where he has bled so many thousands of fish, nor can he bear to see Ingrid's ashen face, so he closes his eye and rows the boat back, jumps onto the quay and runs towards the south of the island, his brothers wide-eyed in astonishment. Then they race after him, closely followed by Benjamin and Jørgen.

Barbro and Daniel help Ingrid and the baby out of the boat and take them up to the house. Barbro also cuts the cord, ties it and stops the bleeding. Ingrid is conscious the whole time and the baby is alive and well, she just needs to look into its eyes.

Barbro understands what she is doing and says that newborn babies' eyes are all the same, the colour develops later, their own individual colour, she knows what she is talking about. And Ingrid notices that the sobbing no longer has her in its grip and she can wait, because it is a girl, her name will be Kaja, and she can see the unmistakeable features, it is the Russian, and the colourless eyes of thousands of innocents killed on the slave ship *Rigel* that everyone has forgotten, the girl's father has been killed too, Ingrid can see that now, Kaja is a child of the *Rigel*.

# 15

God's love for those on the coast is not as great as for those on the mainland and in the towns; for protracted periods He forgets them completely, and *they* forget Him; they might recite a short prayer before eating and heave a sigh over coffee, but when for once He is in a generous mood, they are in no doubt as to where they should direct their thanks. Not that Ingrid folds her hands and raises her eyes to heaven, but now at last she knows, like a cascade of light in total darkness, that if there has been no meaning to anything in the terrible year she has been through, some meaning has now emerged, a flash of hope from a crystalline sky, and she doesn't let the child out of her sight, doesn't miss a single sound or movement, whether Ingrid is asleep or awake, no matter what the time of day the light shines equally brightly in every nook and cranny, despite autumn being well on the way.

Barbro wants to know what she was doing in the færing when the baby was due. Ingrid does, too. Barbro shows her how to breastfeed and tie a nappy so that it is more comfortable for the baby than when Ingrid does it. Ingrid leaves it to her, and Jadviga nods her approval. Barbro is magnificent. She has also started to sing every day now, at Jadviga's request, because of the child and the grass that will grow in the five black-soil gardens in the years to come, because of the son who will soon be returning home, but it also has something to do with Ingrid no longer being half of herself, and it doesn't matter that the child cries, especially at night, it is the roar of the morrow that jars in their ears.

Daniel is paid, he divides the sum between himself and the others according to a formula that gives him considerably more than them, and leaves with the horses and the tools on the new cargo boat, which Ingrid spent her last eider-down money hiring. Both the man leaving and those who remain wave, and their sorrow cannot prevent a temporary peace falling over the island, a peace which is now only disturbed by the continuing homesickness of the Finnmark lads, or at least Arne, a few passing showers and an eagle landing on a rock near the sheep.

So it is time to sort matters out.

They take the key – Ingrid with the baby strapped to her body with one of her mother's thick, flowery shawls, Barbro in her church dress, which she dons even on the most ordinary of days. They open the Lofoten boat shed and drag the three chests into the daylight and view them with critical eyes, they are so old and battered that what once must have been paint on them is now a trail of dust.

One chest belonged to Ingrid's father, the second to her

grandfather and the third to her great-grandfather, the latter is emblazoned with the same initials as her father's: H.B. for Hans Barrøy, and the year 1831. It is also the biggest and least battered of them, for the man was lost at sea at such a young age that his son still hadn't learned to handle a pair of oars.

They ask Arne and his brothers to carry the chest up to the house and put it in the parlour. Benjamin and Jørgen see to the one bearing the inscription Martin Barrøy, 1864. Arne asks what the point is, two Lofoten chests on the floor where the dining table used to be, they had been told to push that up against the closet wall, the chairs stand around like a circle of mute onlookers, it is the end of September.

But now it is the herring season and everything grinds to a halt again.

Ingrid decides they should do the salting themselves instead of gutting fish at the trading post in the shackles of wage labour. Arne and Benjamin agree.

They row to the village in two boats and buy barrels and salt, have it charged to their account by the new foreman with the odd appearance, the one Ingrid sold eider down to, they haggle to get the price as low as they can, they need half-barrels, the windlass on Barrøy can't lift more than that. And that same afternoon they close off the sound between Moltholmen and one of the Lundeskjæret rocks according to Ingrid's instructions, they also set nets westwards from the other rock, thus forming a kind of V, as they have always done here.

However, although they see columns of birds, like roaming

tornadoes, over the sea to the west and north, and also close to the skerries, they don't catch anything until more than a week has passed. But then the nets are almost bursting with fish beneath the new moon, they have to tow them ashore and lose half the catch. But they still have thirteen half-sized barrels. And they are big herring. Ingrid tells the boys to chop off their heads rather than gut them.

Fredrik Barrøy is home from school and is given the job of carrying water and making the brine that is poured into the barrels after they have been laid on their sides. Arne has drilled a hole in the middle of one of the staves on each. Ingrid thinks they should have had a pump on the quay, now they have to carry or winch up buckets of sea water to the rinsing tubs, it is as it has always been, Barrøy has everything, yet lacks something of real importance.

She still carries Kaja on her stomach when she works, it won't be long before Ingrid has her on her back, and now Kaja only screams when she puts her down. Kaja likes movement.

They buy more barrels and salt, set a few more nets, and one afternoon while Suzanne and Ingrid are on the quay in their aprons cutting and carefully layering herring in the barrels, they hear the unmistakeable sounds from the north and see a white crow's nest with the characteristic black ring around its middle slipping past Oterholmen, then the ship itself comes into view, it isn't *Barrøy II*, which they have been waiting for since the decisive letter was sent, but the *Salthammer*.

Only Ingrid recognises it.

They have a wash and stand side by side on the quay, Ingrid with her hands beneath her shawl so that she can warm them on the baby, who gurgles and looks up at her through *Rigel* eyes.

Suzanne spots a familiar figure in the bow with the mooring rope at the ready, she starts jumping up and down and shouting, her hands funnelled to her mouth, Ingrid doesn't move a finger, Lars throws the hawser onto the quay and Helmer slips the loop over the bollard, while Jørgen takes care of the aft mooring rope.

"Is it thi?" she yells down into the boat.

Lars walks down to the deck without answering her, a man in his best years, hair with a pronounced streak of grey, a body that is even more solid and stouter than she remembers, but he is agile and quick on his feet. He positions himself in front of the wheelhouse, where a window is lowered, and the captain, Magnus Mannvik, sticks out his head and casts a fleeting glance up at Ingrid, who nods briefly in response, listens to something Lars says, then disappears into the wheelhouse again, and the engine is turned off.

Lars lifts the companion on the bow deck and shouts down into the cabin. Two young girls in identical dresses, jackets and tights jump out, they also have the same hair and movements, and are the same height, at a sign from Lars they turn and look up at Ingrid and Suzanne, who wave down to them and smile. A woman dressed all in black follows them, a little taller than Lars, she has black hair, too, but with a yellow and white headscarf, which looks like silk in the autumn light. Two boys amble out of the bait house – Ingrid recognises one as Ole – and with them there is an eight- or nine-year-old boy who, she assumes, must be Lars' son, Hans, she frees her hand and waves again, but he doesn't wave back, and Suzanne shouts:

"Hvor's our Felix?"

"Fishen'," Lars says. "Longline fishen'."

He lifts one of the hatches above the hold and is assisted by Magnus – who has come down onto the deck – when he lifts the second. Ingrid hears them discussing which crane to use, and a snatch of laughter. Magnus starts up the engine and yet another woman and boy emerge from the cabin, she is wearing a red skirt and a thick wadmal jacket with an even redder folded woollen collar, she, too, has a headscarf. The two women look around. The one in black interferes in something Magnus is doing with the winch, she watches as a bureau appears unscathed through the hatch and is left dangling by the strap, which Lars hoists up to the winch boom before swinging it over to the quay, and Suzanne yells:

"Hvor's he fishen'?!"

Lars says, th' Thor Iversen Bank, without taking his eyes off the bureau, which slowly descends and lands at Ingrid's feet and stands there in all its glory, on a par with the dresser her father once bought when he had lost his senses, she realises they have come to stay.

She loosens the straps and pulls them from under the piece of furniture so that they can be lifted by the hook that Lars lowers back down into the hold, whence an impressive assortment of trunks, sacks, beds, mattresses, chairs and tables are calmly and ceremoniously winched up and deposited on the stone quay as the future furnishing for two parlours, six bedrooms and two kitchens, a rain shower sweeps over, and the woman in black, who has now stepped ashore, throws a set of oilskins over the bureau and introduces herself as Hanna, curtsies and says she is married to Felix.

Ingrid discovers that she, like the women from Finnmark, has an invisible baby under her clothing, a boy of only one month, Felix's and her third child, Oskar. Suzanne puts a finger in his mouth and realises that the two twin girls are also Felix's, her nieces. She kneels down, helps them up onto the quay and compliments them, in city language, on their nice clothes and the curls in their hair, and shakes their hands and asks them what their names are and tells them her own name and calls Fredrik, who, unperturbed, is walking back down to the shore for two buckets of seawater, they need brine for at least three more barrels.

Hanna resembles one of Ingrid's aunts, who stayed with them once during a crisis, a solemn and deeply religious person, it is written all over her, a strong woman who nonetheless will not be able to survive on her own when the men in her life are gone, Ingrid can see this, and she finds it comforting.

They are told that Felix will be coming on *Barrøy II* some time before Christmas, shortly after the New Year the men have to go back to Lofoten for the new season.

Ingrid turns to Magnus, who has also come onto the quay, and allows him a glimpse of her child, so that he can see there is no more to be said about that matter.

He is polite and pleasant and makes a few comments that, to her annoyance, cause her to blush. She turns to the other woman, who says her name is Selma and is married to Lars, she is as short as he is, but delicate, soft and cheery, with thick, tousled, golden yellow hair. Selma reaches out her hand, and tells her two boys to do the same, Hans is nine and Martin five, and Ingrid can say, well, well, at last we have a Hans and a Martin back on Barrøy and it is only by the skin of her teeth that she manages to prevent her resolution not to shed any more tears from going up in smoke.

However, Barbro has not stopped crying, she interrupted her baking day the second the sounds of the *Salthammer* reached her keen ears in the kitchen, and she has stood still with flour in her hair and on her face and up her bulging arms ever since the bureau was unloaded, staring down at her son, who is operating the windlass and hasn't time to look at her; she has to yell his name through her tears. He answers as a monster of a rust-red armchair swings over her head and lands as softly as a cat beside a dining table:

"Shame on tha, Mother."

Barbro hasn't seen her son for nine years, now she waits patiently until everything has been unloaded, including a great number of interesting items, flour, sugar, three sacks of carrots plus two catering tins of sausages, which Ingrid hasn't seen since before the war, and not least, a pig, cut up and salted in a barrel.

Lars finally comes onto the quay, so Barbro can stand next to him and listen to him talking in irritated tones to Ingrid, talking about something he actually hadn't intended to mention, he claims, but the letter said they would have accommodation ready and waiting for them, and as far as he could see, from where he was standing, there was only a shell of a building with a roof, over in Karvika, and half a boat shed.

Ingrid again feels the ambivalent nature of her relationship with her cousin, the threat combined with the sense of security, but laughs and says it wasn't her who wrote the letter.

"Hva?"

"It war our Suzanne. An' tha mother."

"Felix said nothin' abou' that."

"He war likely heimsick."

Lars plumps down in the armchair and disappears in its embrace, becomes conscious of how small he is and jumps up again. Magnus sits down in his place, he is a much better fit, and says that in that case they will have to move the furniture into the quay house and keep it there until the buildings are finished; it is meant as a joke, but Hanna and Selma exchange glances and one of the twins asks her mother where they are going to live.

"With us," Ingrid replies, turns to Arne and tells him to assemble the boys and go with her.

Back at the house, she takes three burned loaves from the oven, scrapes off the black bits, places them upside down on the table to cool, opens the window and tells Jørgen to fetch the cart. They carry out the two chests and wheel them down to the quay in two trips. There are clothes and cutlery and kitchen utensils in the chest for the Skarsvåg brothers, as well as all the tools and equipment Ingrid can spare, and there are only clothes in the one she sends down with Benjamin and Jørgen. They are also given a rug each, the eight old sheepskins she had left in the barn, a few blankets, some bed linen and the clothes they are wearing, plus the new boots with the soles made from the rubber on the tyres of the German gun carriages.

On the quay, she shouts down to Ole to send the winch hook back up.

From the armchair where he is still sitting Magnus asks what she is doing, there is a bottle of aquavit on one dining table and a circle of small glasses, the others have sat down as though waiting to be served. Ingrid tells him he will have six passengers on his voyage north.

"Who?" Magnus says, getting up.

"You know them," she says.

He lets his eyes wander sceptically over his young travelling companions, smiles when he sees Jørgen and shakes his hand, Benjamin gets a nod and the three brothers one to share.

"I'm going south."

"You'd better drop them off on the mainland then," Ingrid says. "They're going north."

Magnus puts his hands on his hips, looks out to sea and bites his lower lip, glances down at Ole, who gazes enquiringly up at him, and at length manages a nod. Ole stands behind the levers and once again lowers the hook to the quay.

"You called me a bitch last time we were together," Ingrid says as they watch Great-grandfather Barrøy's chest swing into place in the hold.

"Yes, and I meant it," Magnus says.

They smile.

Lars and his sons have lit a fire on the quay, between the stones the rinsing tub usually stands on, the weather is good, he grabs the sledgehammer Arne used on the herring barrels and smashes the lid off one of the catering canisters of sausages, which he places on the fire, and Ingrid remembers how he used to light fires on this precise spot in his younger days when he decided it was too cold to work outside, but couldn't desist. Now he pushes his sons in front of Barbro and says they should say hello to their grandmother, turns quickly back to the bottle on the table, unscrews the cork, fills one of the glasses and offers it to Ingrid.

Ingrid takes it and drinks, almost says "yes" to his unspoken question, whether he is the master of Barrøy now. He pours another glass and gives it to his mother, whose shaking hands spill it. She puts it down again and instead places a hand on each of her grandchildren's heads, then asks her son who the horrible armchair is for.

"It's f' tha, Mother," Lars says, with his back to her, as he fills more glasses.

Ingrid walks up to the house with the two newly arrived

women and shows them where they will be sleeping: Hanna, the baby and the young girls in the South Chamber, Selma in Grandfather's closet, her sons and Lars can sleep in the Swedes' quay house, which has just become vacant, and Suzanne is banished to Ingrid's old childhood room, where Fredrik sleeps.

They slice the loaves Barbro baked and place them together with some newly arrived butter and jam and sweet cheese in a wooden box, and Selma asks who the old woman asleep in the rocking chair is.

"That's Jadviga," Ingrid says.

It has turned dark and the rain is coming down in sheets. The doors of the quay house are open, the flickering light from the fire illuminates the group of people who have moved in the furniture and are sitting around two tables covered in a cloth, as in a restaurant, eating and drinking and talking, it resembles a banquet hall with four bedrooms, two conjoined parlours and two kitchens: Barbro reigns at one end of the long table, with a grandchild under each arm, she doesn't know what to say to them, but she fills their plates with sausages, which they eat with their fingers, and butters their bread, wondering whether to ask if they also like sweet cheese.

Magnus and Lars are sitting next to Ole and his friend at the other end of the table talking about whaling, Lars speculates whether that might be something for him too: hunting minke whales in the midnight sun in the Vestfjord and the Barents Sea, so he doesn't have to idle around in the summer. Magnus says

Lars has land to till, Lars replies that the womenfolk can take care of that, they always have done.

On one side of the table are all the boys from Finnmark, who have just settled into bunks on board the *Salthammer*, and they are wondering whether to join forces when they arrive in the north, this isn't the first time this topic has come up, it isn't far between Mehamn and Skarsvåg; however Jørgen and Benjamin have family waiting for them, they also want to try to trace Jadviga's lost children, and the conversation lapses into a silence it isn't easy to dispel.

Facing them, on the other side, sits Suzanne between her nieces, chatting and serving food and asking them about their father. On either side of them sit Selma and Hanna, eating with a knife and fork and drinking milk and – in Selma's case – aquavit, while Fredrik isn't sitting anywhere, just mooching restlessly around the table, holding the backs of chairs and listening to what is being said, before moving on and listening to the next conversation. He is startled when Lars shouts out:

"Hell, hva's that?"

Something is dripping into his glass. "Is th' roof leaken'?"

Everyone looks up. Arne leans across the table and says he repaired the roof, but ran short of slates, one tile was missing.

They look up at the black sole of a shoe in the rafters, and the drops of water falling from it. Lars gets to his feet and gesticulates, everyone stands up and lifts the tables one metre further north, then sits down again, and Lars places the empty sausage canister on the floor so that they can hear the dripping on the metal, then on the water, until they eventually become soundless, and Fredrik says in his new language:

"Hvor's Ingrid?"

Ingrid is the only person not there. She is lying on her bed in the North Chamber breastfeeding. When Kaja falls asleep, she moves her over to the other side of the bed, so that the little light that penetrates the streaming windowpanes can shine on her face, and time can stop, everything fluid can solidify and Ingrid can try to forget Nelvy.

# 16

Barbro and Hanna had also baked bread and cakes for the day the Finnmark boys were to leave. By then the *Salthammer* had made two trips to the trading post with barrels of herring, and had also collected building materials that Lars paid for with money he had received for the houses he owned in Reine, in cash. And a load of coke, as Ingrid hadn't managed to cut peat in the summer. Magnus Mannvik had got to know Barrøy better, especially the building project in Karvika, which he praised, but not Ingrid, she had gone her own way.

At the moment of departure she shook his hand and thanked him for this and that and the other. He looked as if he had been thinking of calling her a bitch again and adopting a fitting smile, but couldn't find one that was appropriate.

Ingrid also shook hands with Arne, hugged Sverre and told Helmer, who didn't want a hug, that she would miss him. Jadviga was hoisted on board in the massive armchair and placed on the hold hatch, Barbro didn't want it. Magnus lowered the port window in the wheelhouse, stuck his head out and said:

"Well, the weather's behaving," engaged the clutch and the *Salthammer* sailed away.

None of those on board waved, but Jadviga raised a hand. All of those left behind waved, except Fredrik, he was crying, and was laughed at by the new Hans Barrøy, who was told off by both Selma and Suzanne and looked up at his father for support. Lars told him to make friends with Fredrik as quickly as possible, they were going to accompany each other to school and would also be building a house together.

His son laughed scornfully and said something the others wished they hadn't heard, received a stinging clout and he, too, began to cry. Fredrik smirked through his tears.

Then they all walked up to the house.

Lars at Ingrid's side. He said this wasn't going to turn out well.

Ingrid answered they would be making up before too long.

Lars said he wasn't referring to Fredrik, but to the Finnmark boys.

Ingrid reflected on this, and her old feeling of having missed something returned, Lars must have seen something she hadn't. She asked him what he thought about the work they had done in the gardens, he hadn't commented yet, he said it was impressive, and that they would have to get a cow next year. She asked whether it wouldn't be better to have two? He said they would have to see.

With Lars back on Barrøy the milk boat began to call at the island again, even though they didn't have any milk. It brought goods and materials, transported barrels full of herring and empty ones back, they were full-sized barrels now and the fishing was good all month. The boat also brought telegrams from Felix, and one day at the end of September three letters for Ingrid.

It was dreadful weather that day, and she, Kaja and the letters were wet before she got home and could seek refuge in the parlour.

Eva Sofie wrote that she had become engaged to one of the drivers at the hospital, maybe Ingrid could remember him, he had taken her to the boat. Eva Sofie was in the family way, as she put it, was due sometime in the spring, as she also termed it, and the driver was busy repairing her house. But she still didn't trust this peace, she kept thinking about Ingrid, and that gave her no peace of mind . . .

Ingrid tried to manage a smile and hung the letter above the stove to dry.

Eric Falc Johannesen was also thinking about Ingrid, although his letter was little more than reports on the running of the hospital in this new era. But he called her "my child of nature", twice, and wrote that it was a pity he hadn't managed to tame her, an insidious and ambiguous choice of words that embarrassed Ingrid even though she was on her own; she re-read the letter, felt the same discomfort, and put it in the stove.

However, for a few moments she stood looking at the enclosed photograph, of Ingrid and Erik Falc on either side of a Rococo chair in a blossoming apple orchard with her eyes fixed on some invisible point somewhere above her brow. It wasn't difficult to recognise the two people, although neither of them looked like themselves.

She took it into the kitchen and showed it to the others. Suzanne wiped the moisture off it with the back of her hand and studied it, a good-looking man, she said, who was he? Selma said Ingrid looked so young. Hanna thought Ingrid looked frightened and Barbro asked who the lady in the picture was, she didn't recognise the man, either.

Ingrid also hung the photograph up to dry, thinking that one day she would take Kaja to town and have her photograph taken as well, a portrait of mother and daughter, and maybe send a print to someone, but there was no rush, as her child was becoming more and more beautiful with every day that passed. She asked Hanna what this would cost.

"It's expensive," Hanna said.

The third letter was from Arne.

Ingrid is standing on the doorstep one strange evening. What is strange is that it isn't evening but the middle of the day. She sees the milk boat put in, allowing Fredrik and Hans to come ashore, they are home from school, it is Saturday. But she doesn't go down to meet them as she normally does, it is enough to see them racing to be first up to the house. She also spots a figure down by the boat shed, it is Lars.

She asks the boys how school was, but doesn't hear the

answer, instead she walks down and sees that Lars has herded the sheep into the boat shed. She asks him why.

He looks at her, and the child, strokes Kaja's cheek, as if this has anything to do with her.

Ingrid sticks her hand down behind the child, takes the letter from Arne and gives it to him. Lars reads and says:

"Tha gave 'em money?"

Ingrid says yes, she had put Malmberget's leather wallet in the small compartment in the trunk they took with them, the Hans Barrøy 1831 trunk, which Arne thanks them for in more effusive terms than necessary.

"Hva did A say?"

Ingrid shrugs and says nothing.

The letter says that the brothers made it home and found everything in ruins, and pitch black, as expected, since then they had lived in some former barracks in Honingsvåg, and after that in some other barracks in Hammerfest, and were now in Tromsø, at a hospice run by nuns, thanks to the nuns' kindness and Ingrid's money, and they don't know what to do while they wait for spring and the light.

Lars waves the letter and says:

"Hva does *tha* think?"

Ingrid says:

"Tha needs baiters th' comen' winter."

Lars fixes her with his eyes.

"We've got enough of 'em."

"Tha can change 'em."

"Th' one-eyed lad?"

Ingrid decides again not to answer. Lars says:

"Ca' they bait?" Ingrid says:

"They ca' fish."

"We're rowen' on th' seaward side."

"Arne ca' fish thar, the young uns ca' do the baiten'."

Lars gives this some thought, then says blankly that she should write to the brothers and tell them to go to Lofoten and ask for a job at Conrad Hartvigsen's trading post in Reine and tell them to stay in Lars Barrøy's fishing shack over Christmas until he and Felix go north at the beginning of January.

Ingrid looks down at Kaja, who blinks her long, black eyelashes, and she can't bring herself to say "thank you", her eyes wander around the boat shed, and she repeats her question about the sheep.

Lars says:

"Is tha goen' blind?"

He turns his back on her, strides out into the murky day and walks south on his new path to Karvika, it is almost a road now, he is busy.

Ingrid runs after him, but is stopped by an invisible hand and stands looking around, the whole island in one bite, the door that is thrown wide open up at the house and the boys coming out, each holding a slice of bread, they spot Lars and charge over the hill to cut him off, the smoke issuing from the chimney in short, lazy puffs, Barbro emerging and casting sceptical glances to the north and south, pacing towards the clothes rack and removing the garments hanging there so black in the vast silence, the kitchen window opening, Hanna's face and her open mouth, shouting something to Barbro, Barbro turning and answering, it looks like a question, two questions, Ingrid sees it all, half in a daze, the first winter storm is on its way.

Born in Oslo to a family that came from northern Norway, ROY JACOBSEN has twice been nominated for the Nordic Council's Literary Award. He is the author of more than fifteen novels and is a member of the Norwegian Academy for Language and Literature. In 2009 he was shortlisted for the Dublin Impac Award for his novel *The Burnt-Out Town of Miracles*. *The Unseen*, the first of three novels about Ingrid and her family, was a phenomenal bestseller in Norway and was shortlisted for the 2017 Booker International Prize and the 2018 International Dublin Literary Award.

DON BARTLETT is the acclaimed translator of Karl Ove Knausgård's auto-fictional sequence *My Struggle*, as well as of novels by Jo Nesbø and Per Petterson. He lives in Norfolk, England.

DON SHAW is a teacher of Danish and the author of the standard Danish–Thai/Thai–Danish dictionaries. He and Don Bartlett met in university and have collaborated on many translations from both Norwegian and Danish.

## BIBLIOASIS INTERNATIONAL TRANSLATION SERIES

### *General Editor: Stephen Henighan*

1. *I Wrote Stone: The Selected Poetry of Ryszard Kapuściński* (Poland)
Translated by Diana Kuprel & Marek Kusiba

2. *Good Morning Comrades*
by Ondjaki (Angola)
Translated by Stephen Henighan

3. *Kahn & Engelmann*
by Hans Eichner (Austria-Canada)
Translated by Jean M. Snook

4. *Dance With Snakes*
by Horacio Castellanos Moya (El Salvador)
Translated by Lee Paula Springer

5. *Black Alley*
by Mauricio Segura (Quebec)
Translated by Dawn M. Cornelio

6. *The Accident*
by Mihail Sebastian (Romania)
Translated by Stephen Henighan

7. *Love Poems*
by Jaime Sabines (Mexico)
Translated by Colin Carberry

8. *The End of the Story*
by Liliana Heker (Argentina)
Translated by Andrea G. Labinger

9. *The Tuner of Silences*
by Mia Couto (Mozambique)
Translated by David Brookshaw

10. *For as Far as the Eye Can See*
by Robert Melançon (Quebec)
Translated by Judith Cowan

11. *Eucalyptus*
by Mauricio Segura (Quebec)
Translated by Donald Winkler

12. *Granma Nineteen and the Soviet's Secret*
by Ondjaki (Angola)
Translated by Stephen Henighan

13. *Montreal Before Spring*
by Robert Melançon (Quebec)
Translated by Donald McGrath

14. *Pensativities: Essays and Provocations*
by Mia Couto (Mozambique)
Translated by David Brookshaw

15. *Arvida*
by Samuel Archibald (Quebec)
Translated by Donald Winkler

16. *The Orange Grove*
by Larry Tremblay (Quebec)
Translated by Sheila Fischman

17. *The Party Wall*
by Catherine Leroux (Quebec)
Translated by Lazer Lederhendler

18. *Black Bread*
by Emili Teixidor (Catalonia)
Translated by Peter Bush

19. *Boundary*
by Andrée A. Michaud (Quebec)
Translated by Donald Winkler

20. *Red, Yellow, Green*
by Alejandro Saravia (Bolivia-Canada)
Translated by María José Giménez

21. *Bookshops: A Reader's History*
by Jorge Carrión (Spain)
Translated by Peter Bush

22. *Transparent City*
by Ondjaki (Angola)
Translated by Stephen Henighan

23. *Oscar*
by Mauricio Segura (Quebec)
Translated by Donald Winkler

24. *Madame Victoria*
by Catherine Leroux (Quebec)
Translated by Lazer Lederhendler

25. *Rain and Other Stories*
by Mia Couto (Mozambique)
Translated by Eric M. B. Becker

26. *The Dishwasher*
by Stéphane Larue (Quebec)
Translated by Pablo Strauss

27. *Mostarghia*
by Maya Ombasic (Bosnia-Quebec)
Translated by Donald Winkler

28. *Dead Heat*
by Benedek Totth (Hungary)
Translated by Ildikó Noémi Nagy

29. *If You Hear Me*
by Pascale Quiviger (Quebec)
Translated by Lazer Lederhendler

30. *The Unseen*
by Roy Jacobsen (Norway)
Translated by Don Bartlett and Don Shaw

31. *You Will Love What You Have Killed*
by Kevin Lambert (Quebec)
Translated by Donald Winkler

32. *Against Amazon and Other Essays*
by Jorge Carrión (Spain)
Translated by Peter Bush

33. *Sea Loves Me: Selected Stories*
by Mia Couto (Mozambique)
Translated by David Brookshaw
& Eric M.B. Becker

34. *On Time and Water*
by Andri Snær Magnason (Iceland)
Translated by Lytton Smith

35. *White Shadow*
by Roy Jacobsen (Norway)
Translated by Don Bartlett and Don Shaw